"That's ... was...'t enough...
Satisfaction practic...

"Name your price."

"I don't want money. I was trying to explain how much th... estate means to me... I was—"

...n *what* do you want?"

...ook every ounce of her will to stand still, bearing the ...gment in that gaze. The pain in his words cut through ... "I want you to see your father."

... silence that dawned was so tense that Riya felt the ...ion wind around them like a tangible rope. The knot ...is brow cleared, the icy blue of his eyes widened. It ... the last thing he had expected to hear. That she had ...orised him left her only shaking in her leather pumps.

...."

...ing her hands behind her, Riya pushed the words that ...sed to come under his scornful gaze. "Then I won't ... it over. Ever."

... could practically hear him size her up, saw him ...sess his assumptions about her in the way disbelief ... then pity filled his gaze. He looked at her as though ...as seeing her anew.

...n't push me into doing something I don't want to. ...t estate—it's the one thing in the entire world that ...ans something to me."

... words were laden with emotion and so much more. ... she understood that attachment—because she loved ...state too. But she couldn't weaken now...now that ...s here in San Francisco, so close to Robert.

...e already made my decision."

Tara Pammi can't remember a moment when she wasn't lost in a book—especially a romance, which was much more exciting than a mathematics textbook. Years later Tara's wild imagination and love for the written word revealed what she really wanted to do. Now she pairs alpha males who think they know everything with strong women who knock that theory and them off their feet!

Other titles by Tara Pammi available in eBook from www.millsandboon.co.uk:

THE TRUE KING OF DAHAAR
  (A Dynasty of Sand and Scandal)
A DEAL WITH DEMAKIS
THE LAST PRINCE OF DAHAAR
  (A Dynasty of Sand and Scandal)
A TOUCH OF TEMPTATION
  (The Sensational Stanton Sisters)
A HINT OF SCANDAL
  (The Sensational Stanton Sisters)

THE MAN TO BE
RECKONED WITH

BY
TARA PAMMI

Published in Great Britain 2015
by Mills & Boon, an imprint of Harlequin (UK) Limited,
Eton House, 18-24 Paradise Road, Richmond, Surrey, TW9 1SR

© 2015 Tara Pammi

ISBN: 978-0-263-24840-1

Printed and bound in Spain
by CPI, Barcelona

THE MAN TO BE RECKONED WITH

From mathematics class to master's degrees, through crushes on boys to crushing debts, through fights with our moms to marriages and babies—you've always been constant and unflinching in your support and love. This one's for you, Sushma.

PROLOGUE

"HE MIGHT DIE any minute of any day or he might live to be a hundred. There's nothing to be done for it."

Nathaniel Ramirez looked up at the snowy, whitecapped mountain peak and gulped in a big breath. The words he had overheard the cardiologist say to his mother all those years ago reverberated inside his skull. The cold air blasted through his throat, his lungs expanding greedily.

Would this be the day?

He raised his face to the sky as his vision cleared and his heart resumed its normal beat.

At some point during the trek, he had realized he couldn't finish the climb today.

He didn't know whether it was because, after almost twelve years of courting death, he was finally bored of playing hide-and-seek with it, or because he was just plain tired today.

For a decade, he had been on a constant go across the world, without planting roots anywhere, without returning home, making real estate deals in corners of the world, making millions.

An image of the roses in the garden his mother had loved, back in California, their color vividly red, the petals so soft that she had banned him from touching them, flashed across his mind's eye.

A stab of homesickness pierced him as he followed the icy path down. Sweat drenched him as he reached the wooden cabin he had been living in since he closed the Demakis deal in Greece six months ago. Restlessness slithered under his skin.

And he knew what it meant. It meant he was thrashing against the cage he had made for himself; it meant he was getting lonely; thousands of years of human nature were urging him toward making a home, to seek companionship.

He needed to chase a new challenge, whether clinching a real estate deal or conquering a new corner of the world he hadn't stamped with his name yet. Fortunately for him, the world was vast and the challenges it presented numerous.

Because staying still in one place was the one thing that made him weak, that made him long for more than he could have.

He'd just stepped out of a hot shower when his satellite phone beeped. Only a handful of people could reach him via this number. He pushed a hand through his overlong hair and checked the caller ID.

The name flashing on the screen brought an instant smile to his face.

He connected the call, and the sound of their old housekeeper Maria's voice coming down the line filled him with a warmth he had missed for too long. Maria had been his rock after his mom passed.

Suddenly he realized he missed a lot of things from home. He clamped down on the useless yearning before it morphed into the one thing he despised.

Fear.

"Nathan?"

"Maria, how are you?"

He smiled as Maria called him a few names in Spanish and then asked after him as if he were still a little boy.

"You need to come home, Nathan. Your father... It's been too long since you've seen each other."

The last time Nate saw him, his father had been the epitome of a selfish bastard instead of a grieving husband or a comforting father. And despite the decade and the thousands of miles that Nathan had put between them, the bitterness, the anger he felt for him was just as fresh as ever.

Maybe there was no running away from a few things in life.

"Is he ill again, Maria?"

"No. He recovered from the pneumonia. They, at least that woman's daughter, she took good care of him."

Praise from Maria, especially for *that woman's daughter*, as she put it, meant Jackie's daughter had slaved to take care of his dad.

Nathan frowned, the memory of the one time he had seen his father's mistress's daughter leaving a sour taste in his mouth. She had been kind even then.

That day in the garage, with the August sun shining gloriously outside with blatant disregard to the fact that Nathan's entire world had crumbled around him. There had been blooms everywhere, the gardeners keeping it up for his mother even though she had stopped venturing into the garden for months.

The grief that his mother was gone, the chilling fear, the cold fist in his chest that he could drop dead any minute like her, and the little girl who had stood nervously by the garage door, a silent witness to the choking sobs that had racked him.

He hated everything about that day.

"I'm so sorry that your mother died. I can share my mother with you if you want," she had said in a small voice.

And in return, he had ripped through her.

"He's getting married, Nathan." Maria's anxiety cut through his thoughts. "That woman," she said again, refusing to even speak Jacqueline Spear's name, the loathing in her voice crystal clear even through the phone line, "she'll finally have what she wanted, after all these years. Eleven years of living shamelessly with him under his roof..."

Nathan grimaced as Maria spouted a few choice words for Jacqueline Spear. Bitterness filled his veins at the thought of his father's mistress, the woman he had taken up with even before Nathan's mother had passed.

"It's his damn life, Maria. He has every right to spend it as he pleases."

"He does, Nathan. But your mama's house, Nathan... she's preparing to sell it. Just two days ago, she asked me to clean out your mother's room, told me to take anything I wanted. Your mama's belongings, Nathan—all her jewelry's in there. She's putting the entire estate on sale—the grounds, the furniture, the mansion, everything."

Every piece that had been painstakingly put together by his mother with love. And now in the hands of a woman who had been everything his mother hadn't been.

"If you don't come back, it will forever be gone."

Nathan scrunched his eyes closed, and the image of a brick mansion rose in front of him. A strange anger gripped him. He didn't want that house to go to someone else, he realized.

He had lived the life of a loner for a decade, and the image of the house he had run away from hit him hard in his gut. "She doesn't have the right to sell it."

The silence on Maria's end stretched his nerves taut. "He gave it to her, Nathan. As a gift."

Nausea rolled around in his mouth. His father had killed his mother, as clearly as if he had choked the life out of her, with his disgusting affair, and after he'd lived in her house with his mistress and now… His knuckles turned white around the phone.

This he wouldn't, couldn't, tolerate.

No matter that he didn't want to live in the house any more than he wanted to put roots down and settle anywhere in the world.

"He's giving away my mom's house as a wedding gift?"

"Not to Jackie, Nathan. To her daughter, from her first marriage. I don't know if you ever saw her. Your father deeded the house to her a few months ago. After he was dreadfully ill that first time."

Nathan frowned. So Jackie's daughter was selling his mother's house. Getting rid of it for the monetary value it would yield, he supposed.

The restlessness that had simmered inside him a few hours ago dissipated, washed away by furious determination.

It was time to go home. He didn't know how long he would stay or if he could bear to even stay there at all after so many years.

Neither could he let the house, his mother's house, fall into some stranger's grubby hands. He just couldn't.

He bid goodbye to Maria and switched on his laptop.

In a few minutes, he was chatting with his virtual manager, Jacob. He gave orders for a local manager to look after his cabin, for his airline tickets to be booked to San Francisco and last but not the least, for any information the man could dig up on his father's mistress's daughter.

CHAPTER ONE

"I HEARD THE investors sold the company to some reclusive billionaire."

"Someone in HR said he's only bought it for the patented software. That he intends to fire the whole lot of us."

"I didn't realize we had value to attract someone of that ilk."

What ilk? What billionaire?

Riya Mathur rubbed her temples with her fingers, slapping her palms over her ears in a gesture that in no way could silence the useless speculation around her.

What had changed in the week she had been gone for the first time in two years since Drew and she had started the company? What wasn't he telling her?

Her chat window from their internal IM program pinged, and Riya looked down at her screen.

A message from Drew: Come to my cabin, Riya.

Riya felt a knot in her stomach.

Things had steadily been going from bad to worse between her and Drew for six months now. Since New Year's Eve to be exact. And she hadn't known how to make it better except to put her head down and do her job.

Stepping out of the small cubicle she occupied, only separated from the open cabins in the huge hall by one movable shelf, she marched past an anxious, almost hyper group of staff amassed in the break room toward the CEO's cabin. She had spent the better part of the morning waiting on tenterhooks, walking around the different teams and trying to persuade them to get back to work while Drew's door remained resolutely closed.

But his continuing silence, even after an email from her, peppered with little tidbits of gossip, was making her head spin. Running her damp palms over her baggy trousers, she came to a halt at the closed door.

She tapped a couple of times cursorily, and every whisper gathered momentum in pitch and volume. Without waiting for an answer, she turned the handle and the pandemonium behind her descended into a deathly silence.

Stepping inside, she closed the door.

Drew's lean frame was molded by the sunlight streaming through the windows, the San Francisco skyline behind him.

He opened his mouth to speak but stopped abruptly. Her heart in her throat, Riya took a step in his direction. He stiffened a little more and tilted his head.

That same awkwardness that had permeated their every conversation filled the air thickly now.

But this was work. Their company truly had been a product of them both. "The whole office is buzzing with rumors..." She came to a stop a couple of steps from him. "Whatever our personal differences, this is our company, Drew. We're in it together—"

"It was your company until you took the first seed capital from an investor," a new voice, every syllable punctured with a sardonic amusement, said behind her.

Riya turned around so fast she didn't see him for a few seconds. Blinking, she brought her focus back to the huge table and the man sitting at the head of it. The chair faced away from the window. With his long legs sprawled in front of him, only his profile was visible to Riya.

The entire room was bathed in midmorning sunlight and yet the man sat in the one area of the room that the light didn't touch. Ungluing her feet from the spot next to Drew, Riya walked across the room so that she could see better.

She felt the newcomer's gaze on her, studying everything about her. Her usually articulate mind slowed down to a sluggish pace. The feeling that he had been waiting to see *her* tugged at her, a strange little premonition dancing in her gut.

"I've been dying to meet you, Ms. Mathur," he said, turning the vague feeling into solid dread. "The smart mind that built the software engine that drives the company," he added silkily. He had left something else unsaid. She knew it, just as surely as she could feel her heart skidding in her chest.

He had even pronounced her last name perfectly, elongating the *a* after the *M* just right. After knowing her since her freshman year at college, Drew still didn't say it right. It was a small thing, and yet she felt as though this stranger knew her entire history.

Taking the last step past the overfilled bookshelf, Riya came to a halt. Her stomach did a funny dive, her sharp exhale amplified to her own ears.

Her first thought was that he belonged in a motorcycle club and not in a boardroom.

Electric eyes, a brilliant shade of ice blue, set deep in a starkly angled face, collided with hers. That gaze was familiar and strange, amused and serious. A spark of recognition lit up inside her, yet Riya had no idea where she had seen him.

Dark blond hair, so unruly and long that her fingers itched to smooth it back, fell onto his forehead. Copper highlights shimmered in his hair. The sunlight streaming in played hide-and-seek with the hollows of his cheekbones, the planes darker than the hollows. Which meant he spent a lot of time outdoors.

His skin, what she could see of it, was sunburned and looked rough. An untrimmed beard covered his jaw and chin, copper glinting in it too.

That beard, those haphazard clothes, his overall appearance—they should have diluted the intensity of his presence in the small room. It should have made him look less authoritative. Except those eyes negated everything.

They had a bright, alert look to them, a sardonic humor lurking beneath the sharp stare he directed at her.

He wore a dark leather jacket that had obviously seen better days, under which the collar of a faded shirt peeked through.

A cough from behind her brought her up short and Riya felt her cheeks heat up.

Amusement deepened in those eyes.

"Who are you?" The awkwardly phrased question zoomed out of her mouth before she realized. Suddenly it was tantamount that she remember him.

Because she did, Riya realized with a certainty.

He leaned back into his chair, not in the least affected by her tone. There was a sense of contained movement about him even though he remained seated. As though he was forcing his body to do it, as though staying still was an unnatural state for him.

"Nathaniel Ramirez."

Riya's mouth fell open as an article she had read just a few months ago in a travel magazine flashed through her mind's eye.

Luxury Travel Mogul. Virtual Entrepreneur. Billionaire Loner.

Nathaniel Ramirez had been called a visionary in developing hotels that were an extension of the environment, a man who had made millions with zero investment. The string of temporary hotels, which he'd envisioned and built with various landowners in different parts of the world, were all the rage for celebrities who wanted a private vacation, away from prying eyes.

He had tapped into a market that not only had met an existing demand but had opened a whole new industry to the local men in so many remote corners of the world.

And more than any of that, he was an enigma who'd traveled the world over since he was seventeen, didn't stay in one place past a few months, didn't own a home anywhere in the world and worst of all, had no family ties or relationships.

Even the magazine hadn't been able to get a picture of him. It had been a virtual interview.

The quintessential loner, the magazine had called him, the perfect personality for a man who traveled the world over and over. The fact that he made money doing it was just a perk, someone had heard him remark.

He'd only said his name, and nothing more about what he was doing here, in San Francisco, in Travelogue, in their start-up company's headquarters.

Why? Why would he give his name instead of stating why he was here?

She threw a quick look behind her and noticed Drew still stood unmoving at the bay windows, his mouth tight, his gaze swinging between her and Mr. Ramirez.

"You make a living out of traveling the world. What can a small online travel sales company do for you?" She shot Drew a look of pure desperation. "And why are you sitting in Drew's chair?"

The intensity of his gaze, while nothing new to Riya,

still had a disconcerting element to it. Men stared at her. All the time.

She had never learned how to handle the attention or divert it, much less enjoy it, as Jackie did. Only painstakingly cultivated an indifference to those heated, lingering looks. But something about him made it harder.

Finally he uncoiled from his lounging position. And a strange little wave of apprehension skittered through her.

"I bought controlling interest in Travelogue last night, Ms. Mathur."

She blinked, his soft declaration ringing in her ears. "I bought a gallon of milk and bread last night."

The sarcastic words fell easily from her mouth while inside, she struggled not to give in to the fear gripping her.

"It wasn't that simple," Nathan said, getting up from the uncomfortable chair. The whole cabin was both inconvenient and way too small for him. Every way he turned, there was a desk or chair or a pile of books ready to bang into him. He felt boxed in.

Walking around the table, he stopped at arm's length from her, the fear hidden under her sarcastic barb obvious. Gratification filled him even as he gave the rampant curiosity inside him free rein.

Like mother, like daughter.

He pushed the insidiously nasty thought away. True, Riya Mathur was the most beautiful woman he had ever seen, and as a man who had traveled to all the corners of the world, he'd seen more than his share.

She was also, apparently, extremely smart and as possessed of the talent for messing with men's minds as her mother, if everything he had heard and Drew Anderson's blatantly obvious craze for her was anything to go by.

But where Jacqueline met the world with a devil-may-care attitude, flaunting her beauty with an irreverent smile, her daughter's beauty was diluted with intelligence and a carefully constructed air of indifference.

Which, he realized with a self-deprecating smile, made every male of the species assume himself equal to the task of unraveling all that beauty and fire.

Exquisite almond-shaped, golden brown eyes, defiant, scared and hidden behind spectacles, a high forehead, a straight, distinctive nose that hinted at stubbornness and a bow-shaped mouth. All this on the backdrop of a golden caramel-colored silky smooth complexion, as though Jackie's alabaster and her Indian father's brown had been mixed in perfect proportions.

She had dressed to underplay everything about herself, and this only spurred him on to observe more. It was like a cloud hovering over a mountaintop, trying to hide the magnificence of the peak beneath it.

A wary and puzzled look lingered in her eyes since she had stepped inside. Which meant it was only a matter of time before she remembered him.

Because he had changed his last name, and he looked eons different from the sobbing seventeen-year-old she had seen eleven years ago.

He should just tell her and get it over with, he knew. And yet he kept quiet, his curiosity about her drumming out every other instinct.

"I had to call in a lot of favors to find your investors. Once they were informed of my intent, they were more than happy to accommodate me. Apparently they're not happy with the ways things are being run."

"You mean disappointed about the bucket loads of money they want us to make?" A flash of regret crossed her face as soon as she said it.

She was nervous, which was what he'd intended.

"And that's wrong how, Ms. Mathur? Why do you think investors fund start-ups? Out of the goodness of their hearts?"

"I don't think so. But there's growth *and* there's risk." She took a deep breath as though striving to get herself under control. "And if it's profits that you're after, then why buy us at all?"

"Let's just say it caught my fancy."

Frustration radiated out of her. "Our livelihood, everything we've worked toward the past four years is hanging in the balance. And all you're talking about is late night shopping, things catching your fancy. Maybe living your life on the periphery of civilization all these years, cut off from your fellow man, traipsing through the world with no ties—"

"Riya, no...." She heard Drew's soft warning behind her. But she was far too scared to pay heed.

"—has made you see only profit margins, but for us, the human element is just as important as the bottom line."

"You make me sound like a lone wolf, Ms. Mathur."

"Well, you are one, aren't you?" She closed her eyes and fought for control. "Look, all I care about is what you intend to do with the company. With us."

Something inched into his features, hardening the look in his eyes. "Leave us alone, Mr. Anderson."

"No," Riya said aloud as Mr. Ramirez walked around the table and toward her. Panic made her words rushed. "There's nothing you have to say to me that Drew can't hear."

Stopping next to her, Drew met her gaze finally. The resignation in his eyes knocked the breath out of her as nothing else could. "Drew, whatever you're thinking, we can fight this. We own the patent to the software engine—"

"Does nothing else matter to you except the blasted company? Statues possess more feelings than you do."

Bitterness spewed from every word, and the hurt festering beneath them lanced through her. She paled under his attack, struggled to put into words why.

"I'm done, Riya," Drew said, with a hint of regret.

"But, Drew, I…"

His hands on her shoulders, Drew bent and kissed her cheek, all the while the deep-set ice-blue gaze of the arrogant man who was kicking Drew out stayed on her without blinking.

Something flitted in that gaze. An insinuation? A challenge? There one minute, chased away by a cool mockery the next.

But Riya didn't look away. Locking her hands by her side, she stood frozen to the spot.

Stepping back from her, Drew turned. "I'll set up something with your assistant, Nathan."

Without breaking her gaze, the hateful man nodded.

"Goodbye, Riya."

The words felt so final that Riya shivered.

Leaving her flailing in the middle of the room, Drew closed the door behind him. It felt as if she were locked in a cage with a wild animal even as her mind was sifting and delving deeper.

Nathan…Nathan…Nathaniel Ramirez. Owns a group of travel and vacation companies called RunAway International, has traveled the world since he was seventeen…

A strange shiver began at the base of her spine, inched everywhere. She pushed her fingers through her hair, a nervous gesture she had never gotten over. "What did Drew mean?"

"Mr. Anderson decided he wanted to move on. From…"

His gaze swept over her, a puzzle in it. "...*Travelogue*," he finished, leaving something unsaid.

Riya felt as if he had slapped her. He had said so much without saying anything, and she couldn't even defend herself against what she didn't understand. She had never felt more out of her depth. "Who the hell do you think you are? And you can't just kick him out. Drew and I own—"

"He sold his share of the stock. To me. I now own seventy-five percent of your company. I'm your new *partner*, Riya. Or boss, or really...there are so many things we could call each other."

CHAPTER TWO

AND JUST LIKE that, her name on his lips, spoken like a soft invocation, unlocked the memory her mind had been trying to grasp from the moment she looked into that ice-blue gaze.

"She's dead. And she died knowing that your trashy mother is just waiting at the gates, ready to come in and take her place. I hope you both rot in hell."

The memory of that long-ago day flashed through her so vividly that Riya had to grab the chair to steady her shaking legs.

Robert's wife had been Anna. Anna Ramirez.

Little shivers spewed all over and she hugged herself. She had brought this on herself. "You're Nathan Keys. You're Robert's son. I read about you and I never realized..."

He nodded and Riya felt her breath leave her in a big rush.

Her little lie had worked and here he was, with the largest of her company's stock, her livelihood in his hand.

Robert's son, the boy who had run away from home after his mother's death, the son of the married man with whom her mother had taken up, the son of the man who had been more a father to her than her own had ever been.

The son she had been trying to bring back to Robert.

She had lied to Maria about selling the estate, hoping it would lure him back home. Thought she would give Nathan a chance she had never had with her own father.

A hysterical laugh rose through her.

Leaning against the far wall, his legs crossed together in casual elegance, he smiled, his tanned skin glinting in contrast against the white of his teeth. "What? No 'welcome home' greeting for your almost stepbrother, Riya?"

There were so many things wrong about his fake greeting, the worst of which was how aware she was of him in the small room. Mortification drenching her inside, Riya glared at him. "You're kidding me, right?"

"My acceptance of your offer for familial solidarity is almost a decade late, but—"

Her chest fell and rose as she fought for a breath. "You... you *waltz* in here, get rid of my business partner, wave the biggest chunk of my company in my face—" she pushed her shaking fingers through her hair "—and you want welcome?"

He stayed silent and her stride ate up the distance between them. Fear was a stringent pulse in her head. "If this is revenge for my mother's affair with your father, let me tell you—"

"I don't give a damn about your mother *or* my father."

The very lack of emotion in his words stilled Riya's thoughts. He was going to be livid when he learned what she had intended. "Then what is this?"

"You refused every offer I had my lawyers put forward for the sale of the estate."

Her gut twisting with fear, Riya flopped into a chair. Hiding her face in her hands, she fought through it. He had moved to acquire her company because she refused his escalating offers for the sale of the estate.

What would he do when he learned she had never intended to sell it in the first place? What had she brought on herself?

Nathan stared at the lustrous swath of dark brown hair that fell like a curtain over Riya. Even as impatience pulled at him, he stood transfixed, stunned anew by the sharpness of his reaction to her.

Every minute they spent in this confining room, his awareness of her grew like an avalanche that couldn't be stopped.

How she wore no makeup and yet the very lack of it only heightened her beautiful skin and sharp features.

How everything about her beauty was underplayed like her professional but bland brown dress shirt and trousers.

And how utterly she failed at masking that beauty.

How exquisitely expressive her wide, almond-shaped eyes were and how she fluttered those long lashes down when she wanted to hide her expression.

Her slender shoulders trembled and he felt a pang of regret. "All I want is the estate. However high I went, you kept refusing my offers. Refused to even give a reason."

She looked up, the flash of fear in her eyes still just as obvious. But now there was a resolve too. "So you made a play for my company?"

"Yes. It's called leverage. Believe me, as innovative as your software engine is, your little company is not Run-Away International material. Sign on the dotted line today and you'll leave here a rich woman. I'll even leave you to run your boring company. Of course, you'll run it into the ground in two years the way you're going, but being the uncaring bastard that I am, I'll let you ruin your and your staff's future."

"What about all the money you spent on acquiring it?"

"A drop in the ocean. I'm sure the stock will be worthless in a couple of years anyway."

Riya chafed at his grating confidence that she would only ruin the company. But she couldn't focus on that now, and there was no good way to put it.

"I didn't accept those offers because I never intended to sell the estate *to anyone*. I still don't."

"Then why did Maria assume that…"

Every inch of his face tightened as if it had been poured over by concrete and had permanently set with the fury in those chilling eyes. He was still leaning against the table, and yet he looked as if the seams of his control would burst any second.

But he didn't move, didn't lose control even by the flicker of a muscle. Only the sheer frost in his gaze was testament to the fury in his eyes. Finally he blinked and Riya felt the tightness in her chest relent infinitesimally.

The most unholy glint appeared in his eye, sending a ripple of apprehension through her.

"You manipulated Maria and me." His words rang with awe and derision, his gaze studying her, as if he was reevaluating and coming to an unsavory conclusion. He moved toward her slowly. "You laid bread crumbs very cleverly to make sure I trailed after you."

"Yes."

The single word sounded like a boom in the wake of his silent chill.

"You took advantage of my attachment to that estate. You knew I would go as high as you wanted."

Forcing a laugh, which sounded as artificial as it felt, she took a step back, her nerves stretching tighter and tighter.

"Actually I took advantage of your hatred for me and Jackie." And because his silence confirmed it, she continued, battling the ugly truth. "I wasn't even sure it would work. Maria just barely tolerates me. How would I know she would come tattling to you?"

Shaking his head, he covered another step. Though it was cowardly, Riya couldn't stop herself from stepping back again. "Don't minimize your accomplishment now. You knew exactly what you were doing."

Heat flamed her cheeks. "Fine. Something she had said a few months ago stuck with me. About how you might have considered coming back long ago if only Jackie and I were gone. About how much you loved the estate, even the staff, and how dare Robert give it to me? About how I was stealing even this from you."

"So you decided luring me here would make you the maximum amount of money on the estate."

"That's not true. I felt guilty. I never asked Robert for the estate. I know it's not—"

"And your guilt, your insecurities give you the right to play games with me?"

The depth of his perception awed Riya. Despite constantly reminding herself that she had been too young to change anything, she had remembered his grief-stricken words again and again, felt guilt carve a permanent place inside her gut.

His gaze met hers, an icy resolve in it, and Riya forgot what she had been about to say. There was not an inch of that grief-stricken boy in him. Only a cold fire, an absolute detachment.

He reached her, and her heart slammed against her rib cage. She couldn't blink, couldn't look away from that piercing blue. And a slow tremor took root in her muscles. Like the time when she'd had the flu. Only in a less hurting and more disconcerting way. As if every fiber of her were a stringent pulse vibrating in tune to his every move.

His lean body neatly caging her against the alcove, his gaze was a fiery frost. "Why are you doing this?"

"You were gone for eleven years. Eleven years during which time I helped Robert with the administration of the estate, with the staff, with everything. You were off doing who knows what and I slogged over every account, every expense and income number, in the face of a staff that hated the very sight of me. I did everything I could to keep that place going." She had tried to be a model daughter to Robert and Jackie, had taken care of him when he fell sick.

Nothing she had done had removed the shadows of guilt and ache in Robert's eyes.

"That's what this is all about? What I offered wasn't enough?" Nathan said, coming closer. Satisfaction practically coated every word. "Name your price."

"I don't want money. I was trying to explain how much that estate means to me...I was—"

"Then what the hell do you want? How dare you manipulate me after your mother turned my mother's last few days into the worst of her life?"

It took every ounce of her will to stand still, bearing the judgment in that gaze. The pain in his words cut through her. "I want you to see Robert."

The silence that dawned was so tense that Riya felt the tension wind around them like a tangible rope. The knot in his brow cleared, the icy blue of his eyes widened. It was the last thing he had expected to hear. That she had surprised him left her only shaking in her leather pumps.

"No."

Fisting her hands behind her, Riya pushed the words that refused to come under his scornful gaze. "Then I won't sign it over. Ever."

She could practically hear him size her up, reassess his assumptions about her in the way disbelief and then pity filled his gaze. He looked at her as though he was seeing her anew.

"Don't lose what you've built trying to alleviate some weird guilt. Don't push me into doing something I don't want to. That estate, it's the one thing in the entire world that means something to me."

His words were laden with emotion and so much more. And she understood that attachment, because she loved the estate too. But she couldn't weaken now, now that he was here in San Francisco, so close to Robert.

"I've already made my decision."

He ran his fingers through his overlong hair, his gaze a winter frost. There was a tremble in the taut line of his shoulders, a hoarse thread in his tone when he spoke. "I'll drag you through the courts. Your company, I'm going to tear it to pieces. Is it still worth it?"

Riya swayed, the impact of what he was saying sweeping through her with the force of a gale. To see her company pulled apart and sold for pieces... Every inch of her revolted at the mere thought. Desperation filled her words.

"I deceived you. My staff has nothing to do with this. Can you be so heartless to take away their jobs?"

Their gazes locked and held. And every second felt like an eternity to her.

Finally he spoke, his mouth a tight line. "Yes."

The fight deflated out of Riya and she held herself together by sheer will. Her company was everything to her. But if Robert hadn't been there for her when she needed an adult with a kind word, Riya couldn't bear to imagine what her life would have been today.

"Fine. The estate, it's rightfully yours, I believe that. And eventually it will be. But a legal battle will take years.

Robert said he made sure the deed was ironclad, exactly to avoid this kind of battle if he died suddenly."

"Because he's determined to rob even this from me?"

"No. You're misunderstanding him. He thought he was going to die. He... A long, drawn-out court battle is what you want for your mother's house? For Maria and the staff who have looked after the house all these years, for your mother's memory?"

His jaw flexed tight, the vein in his temple flickering threateningly. "You have no right to speak of her."

The utter loathing in his words slashed through her. Because he was right. His fury was justified.

She had no right to even speak of his mother, no right to her estate. To this day, she was equal parts amazed and perplexed that Robert had even deeded it to her.

For the first time in her life, she truly wished she was more like her mother—carefree, blissfully ignorant of everything around her but her own happiness. Wished she could turn her back on this man who threatened everything she had built, wished she could turn her back on the shadows that haunted Robert's eyes.

"I've no right to speak of her, true, but I'm sure she would never have wanted you to hate him all your life. Everyone's always talking about what a generous and kind lady she was and—"

He flinched as though she had laid a hand on him. "You have no idea what she'd have wanted." He stood at the window, just as Drew had done, his wide frame blocking the sunlight from coming in. Contrary to the cold, heartless man she had called him, he looked like a volcano of simmering emotions.

"Get out. I have nothing more to say to you."

Riya closed the door behind her, her legs shaking. Panic pounded through her.

Would he break Travelogue into pieces? How could she fight to keep what was hers? How was she to convince him that it was only Robert's haunting pain that had driven her to this?

Her head reeling, she stepped into the huge, open area laid out with open cabins.

The staff had already figured out that Drew was gone. The faint scraping and shuffling of chairs, the concerned glances in her direction—they were looking to her to provide some direction.

But Riya had no way to save the day, no answer to give to those hopeful looks. She grabbed her handbag and left, unable to think of anything else but temporary escape.

Nathan stared at the closed door, still trying to control his raging emotions. One flimsy, fragile woman had so nearly eroded his self-control.

It had taken him a few years to get over the grief of his mother's death, to accept the fatality of his own condition. He'd been so scared, alone and he'd lashed out at the world.

But in the end, he had not only accepted it but also tailored his life to live it without being haunted by the fear of dying every minute. Had made sure he'd not formed an attachment to anyone, made sure that no relationship could leave him weak. Like the way it had left his mother in the end.

Had gloried in each day he had, lived it to the fullest.

Today, he hadn't been able to help himself from taunting the manipulative minx, from pushing her. But for all the steely will with which she had manipulated him, there was a naiveté to her that cooled his interest. In a million years, he wouldn't have expected his father to command such loyalty in anyone. So much that she was risking everything she owned.

But nothing he did or could do would shake that resolve. Despite the very clever way she had manipulated Maria and taken advantage of his attachment to the estate, he had to admire that resolve. And she was right about one more thing.

Engaging his father in a legal battle would gain him nothing but a deadlock for years to come. He would win in the end, but when, he didn't know.

Time was the one thing that Nate didn't have the luxury or certainty of.

He wanted that estate, and convincing Riya to sell it back to him as soon as possible would be the biggest win of his life. He couldn't dismantle her company for no good reason, couldn't just play with the livelihood of so many people.

But he had learned enough about the smart, steel-willed beauty. Just the thought of those beautiful eyes widening with awareness and shock, the way she held herself rigid when he had neared her, brought a smile to his face.

He was going to enjoy convincing her to sell the estate to him.

CHAPTER THREE

BY THE TIME Riya drove past the electronically manned gates and along the gravel driveway lined with the tall century-old oaks, she was still wondering what she would say to Jackie or how she would bring up the subject of Nathan. Jackie had the most singular way of looking at the world and the people in it. Only interested in how they affected her own life and happiness.

Riya pulled the window down and took a deep breath. The smell of pine needles and the fragrance of the roses greeted her.

The sight of the mansion emerging just as the driveway straightened always revived her, filled her with an indescribable joy. For her, the brick mansion meant home.

Driving around the courtyard, she pulled into the garage, parked and leaned her forehead on the steering wheel. Disappointment and a perverse anger filled her. Nathan didn't love the estate as she did, had been gone for a decade without a thought for it.

Would probably kick them all out, *her especially*, without a second thought. And to leave this place, to say goodbye finally? The very thought made her chest hurt.

Grabbing her laptop bag and her handbag, she stepped out of her car. All she wanted was to have a bath and sink into her bed and deal with everything tomorrow. She entered the vast, homely kitchen through the back door intending to go up quietly when Jackie called her.

Dressed in a cream silk pantsuit, she looked perfectly put together, as always. Except for the frown marring her brow.

"Riya! I've been calling you for hours and you didn't answer a single time." Her painted mouth trembled. "He's here, just…appeared out of thin air, after all these years."

Riya froze, her gaze flying around the house, her heart ratcheting in her chest. Fighting the rising panic, because of course it had always fallen to her to be the calm one, she straightened her spine. "Mom," she said loudly. "Calm down."

She called her that so infrequently now that Jackie looked at her with alarm.

"Now tell me clearly what happened."

"Nathaniel is here," her mother said, awe coating her words. "Apparently he's some big-shot billionaire who can ruin us with one word or—"

"He said that to you?"

"Of course not. He won't even meet my eyes. It's as if I'm not there, standing right in front of him. That witch Maria said it. He looks so different too, all lean and so coldly distant and arrogant."

Riya nodded, surprised that Jackie had noticed it too. There was something she couldn't pinpoint about Nathan either. A sort of cool detachment, a layer of frost as if nothing or no one could touch him. And yet he had been so angry when she refused to sign over the estate.

"Even Maria took a few seconds to recognize him. He just stood there looking as if he owned the place, when he didn't even ask after Robert all these years." Riya bit the inside of her cheek to keep from correcting her mother that the estate *was* his. "He arrived a couple of hours ago. Showed up at the front door and sent the staff into a frenzy.

They were all crying and laughing, and Robert's not even in town. He won't say why he's here."

How? She hadn't even seen his car in the garage. "Where is he? Did he say what he wants?"

"He's been wandering around the estate, drops in every half hour or so. Maria said he wants to see you."

Riya's heart sank to her feet.

A calculating look emerged in her mother's eyes, her panic forgotten. "Why *is* he looking for you? I'm still shaking from the shock of seeing him, and all this time, if you'd known that he was—"

"Hello, Riya."

Every time he said her name, it was like flipping a switch on inside her. A caress. An invitation. For what, she didn't even want to speculate. Her skin tingling, Riya turned.

He stood at the huge arched entrance into the kitchen.

Once again, Riya felt the impact of his presence like a magnet pulled toward a slab of iron.

The beard was still unshaved, but he had changed. Now his clothes reflected the casual power he exuded so easily. The rumpled shirt had been exchanged for a white dress shirt and a formal jacket this time. The snowy-white collar a contrast against his sunburned skin. His hair gleamed with wetness, looked more black than brown.

He looked knee-meltingly gorgeous. Case in point, her knees practically buckled beneath her.

"You didn't come back to the office, haven't been answering my calls," he said, waving his cell phone.

"I didn't realize I was supposed to be at your beck and call," she retorted, not trusting the invasive intimacy of his smile. In fact, she had liked him better when he was angry and threatening. "Not everything I do is about you."

That small smile turned into a grin, and his teeth gleamed against his tanned skin. It lit up his whole face,

softening the harsh angles of his features. And the mouth…
she had been right. It was made for smiling and something
else that she didn't want to think about.

"From now on, it's going to be all about me," he said,
stretching his arms by his sides. The casual gesture drew
her gaze to the breadth of his shoulders. That jacket was
cut perfectly, following the wide swath of his shoulders and
the narrowing of his waist.

Alarm spiked through her. "No."

"I have a proposition for you." Something glimmered
in his gaze. "You're not chickening out already, are you?"

Jackie gasped, and Riya wondered if her mother could
explode from the tension radiating from her. She infused
steel into her voice. "We don't have a deal."

"We do now. You've…*persuaded* me to take a chance
on you, Riya."

There was no way to arrest the heat blooming up her
face. He was doing it on purpose. Saying her name like that,
insinuating with that smile that there was more between
them than his hatred and her risky gamble. She wanted to
run away and hide in her bedroom, hope it was all a bad
dream.

Next to her, Jackie began again. "Riya, how dare you
not tell me—"

Nathan shot Jackie a look. Pure arctic frost, it was the
only way Riya could describe it. Granted, he probably was
the one man who could shut Jackie up without meaning to,
but Riya had a feeling he would have the same effect on all
of them, even if he had just been Nathaniel Ramirez. And
not the adored heir of the estate.

He had that kind of a presence. Contained and con-
trolled with a violent energy brimming underneath the
calm facade.

How was it possible that she could notice so much, understand so much about him just in a few hours?

"Come," he said in a cajoling tone as if she were a recalcitrant child. When she still didn't move, he caught her wrist and tugged.

Her bare skin tingling at the contact of his rough fingers, Riya followed, past the nonplussed staff, who had gathered in the huge dining hall, and her pale mother, through the door and out into the lush acreage behind the house.

A cold breeze blew her hair in her face, and with a soft huff, Riya pulled it all to the side. The night was inky black, only the moon and carefully placed lights on the ground illuminating the path for them.

But instead of dulling his presence, the dark intensified her awareness of him. The graceful line of his shoulders, the taper of his lean chest to his waist and the corded energy of his thighs when she stumbled and he steadied her.

Her own senses revolted against her mind, determined to observe and absorb every little thing about him. They'd reached the well-lit-up gazebo in the south corner of the estate when Riya realized his long fingers were still wrapped around her wrist.

Dragging her feet on the grass, she tugged her hand away.

The splish-splash of water from another fountain, the relentless whisper of the cicadas, a hundred different fragrances carried around by the breeze greeted her. The very place she had always found blissfully peaceful was now ruined by the man playing a cat-and-mouse game with her livelihood. And something much worse.

Grasping the fear that was the only way to puncture her awareness of him, she lashed out. "You couldn't have given me an evening to brace myself? Let me figure out how and what I'm going to tell my mother, to figure out my future?"

"You left without a word to anyone. Is this how you run the company?"

"The very company that you threatened to tear into pieces?" she threw at him. "You asked me to get out. Very clearly."

"You were blackmailing me."

She bristled at the outrage in his voice. "I was doing no such thing." And because she couldn't bear to simply stop thinking of it as her company, she continued. "Even if your plan is to dismantle the company and sell it for bits, you'll need a skeleton staff to see through the memberships for the rest of the year. I recommend you keep Sam Hawkins on. He's been there from the beginning and Martha Gomez too. She needs this job and she'll be invaluable to—"

All of her panic ground to a halt as his long-limbed stride ate the distance between them.

"I don't remember firing you. Are you resigning, then?"

Riya reached behind her and grasped the wooden column. But there was nowhere to go and he was standing too close.

The lights from around the gazebo cast him in shadows.

Close enough to realize how many different shades of blue his eyes could turn depending on the light. Close enough for her to see the shape of his mouth, which had a hint of gaiety to it. Close enough for her to breathe and learn the scent of him and realize why he affected her so much.

She had never before experienced the weird pull in her stomach, the feverish tremble that gripped her, the constant fascination with every aspect of him.

Fisting her hands by her sides, she clamped down the shaky realization.

His gaze rested on her mouth for a nanosecond. Only an infinitesimal fragment of time, but her lips tingled. "I didn't quit. But have you left me a choice?"

As if the tension became too much even for him, he moved to her side and leaned against the structure. "The staff's murderous glares after you left would have turned me into dust if I hadn't told them you were just having a tantrum."

Her breath left her in a huge whoosh, the sound amplified in the silence. "Building up their hopes that everything's okay is just cruel. Does nothing get to you?"

"No."

His response wasn't threatening or emotional. Scarily, it was honest.

His watch glinted in the light as he folded his hands. "I'll give you and your staff one chance. Prove that Travelogue and you are worth taking on as part of RunAway International."

Catching the immediate thanks that rose to her lips, she turned toward him. Her heart thumped hard in her chest. Whether it was because of how close he was standing or because he was giving her a chance, she had no idea.

Ruthlessly killing her own hopes, she shook her head. "I don't want to work for you."

"Why not?"

"What do you mean *why not*?" She moved away, exasperated by him and her reaction to him. "Because you and I have a history, that's why. And not a good one. Whatever you think of me, I lied because…"

He gave her such an arch look that she backpedaled quickly. "Fine. I manipulated Maria and you with good intentions. Whereas you…you are doing this out of some twisted need for *revenge*. That's it. You want to torture me, guilt me and then—"

He grinned, and his blue eyes glittered. Her knees wobbled. "Have you always been this prone to drama or is it me that brings it out in you?"

How she wanted to say he affected her in no way, but they would both know she was lying. Better instead to focus on fighting it. "Why the sudden change of heart, then?"

"A strong sense of familial duty? A core made of kindness?"

Rolling her eyes, she swatted him. Deftly, he caught her hand in his.

Her breath stuck in her throat. Her fingers moved over his in the dark, registering the different texture of his palm—rough and abrasive, devoid of any softness, so different from her own.

It was his absolute stillness next to her, just as powerful as that latent energy, that made her realize what she was doing.

She jerked her hand away, the air she had been holding rushing out of her.

What the hell was she doing, *pawing* him like that? He was her employer, her enemy...

No man had been so dangerous to her internal balance as him. No man had ever spun her senses so easily.

Rubbing shaking fingers over her face, she struggled to think back to their conversation. "You're agreeing to see Robert, then?"

"If you give me a date now as to when you will sign the deed over to me."

"Stay here in San Francisco until their wedding. See Robert, let him speak to you. And I'll sign over the estate the day after the wedding. Also, none of my staff will be made redundant. When this is all over, I want you to go away and leave Travelogue alone. Forever."

"That depends on if Travelogue stays intact that long."

"If you give us a fair chance, I have no doubt it will."

His eyes gleamed ferociously. "You've got a lot of nerve, setting conditions to sell my mother's house back to me."

"You're a billionaire, you're your own boss and as far as I understand, you have no one in your life that you're answerable to. What's two months in the big picture of your life, Nathan?"

"Everything, Riya." There was no humor in his smile now, only a dark warning. "This is your last chance to let it go."

She didn't take even a beat to think it over. "No. Robert... he...I'll do anything for him."

His curious silence swathed her and Riya felt like the rabbit in the story her father had told her when she was little. The rabbit had gone into the lion's den, determined to change his mind about eating one animal every day.

At that point, she had stuck her fingers in her ears and begged him not to continue. A few days after that, she and Jackie had left. Her father had never seen her again, never called her, never sent a birthday card.

For years, she had wondered if he thought of her, hoped he would write to her, call Jackie to ask about her.

Only utter and absolute silence had greeted her hopes.

Now...now she didn't even remember his face clearly. On the road with Jackie, hearing her crying at night, not knowing where they would go next—it had been the most uncertain time of her life. Until Jackie had met Robert and he had taken them to his estate, Riya had thought she would never know a stable home again.

And to see Robert ache to see Nathan, to speak a few words to him, she couldn't back down now. Not when Nathan was finally here.

"Fine. Come to work Monday morning."

She saw the shadow of something in his eyes—a promise, a challenge.

"I'll stay two months. I'll even dance with you at the wedding."

"I don't want to dance with—"

"You started this, Riya. I'm going to finish it."

She breathed in cold gulps of air, only then seeing the faint shape of a chopper. "Stop saying my name like that," she said, not sure when the words had exactly left her lips.

Frowning, he stepped closer. "Am I saying it wrong?"

There was that strange little tension again. Winding around them, tugging at them.

"No. I just…we're…"

The helicopter blades began whirring, and he bent toward her to make himself heard. A firestorm danced through Riya as his breath played on her nape.

It was a heated brand, a molten caress. The simple touch of his fingers on her waist as she swayed seared through the cotton of her shirt.

"Mr. Ramirez and Ms. Mathur are too formal when we're going to work in close quarters for a couple of months. And calling each other brother and sister, especially when we…" Her heart drummed in her ears, a flash of heat bursting all over her as he paused dramatically. "…*obviously don't like each other* will just earn us a place on a daytime soap opera, don't you think?

"Nathan and Riya, it has to be."

She felt his smile instead of saw it, the faint graze of his beard against her jaw making her hyperaware of him. He lifted his head and Riya stared mutely at the striking beauty of the planes of his face.

All wicked, from the twinkle in his eyes to the dimples in his cheeks. And sexy all the way.

"See you Monday morning." He stepped back, sending

her heart pitter-pattering all over her chest. "And FYI, I'm what they call an exacting boss."

By the time Riya walked the long way around the acreage back to the house, she was hungry and tired and her head hurt.

Turning the gleaming antique handle on the side door into the kitchen, she stepped in. Even though her stomach rumbled, all she wanted was to get into bed and forget that this day had happened.

She couldn't believe that Drew had sold her out so easily, couldn't believe what she had set in motion. And of all things, she couldn't believe the sharp and stringent quality of her awareness of Nathan, of his every word and gesture, of the flash of the same awareness in his. But she had no doubt, where she was floundering and flailing in the wake of it, it was nothing but a game to him.

The overhead ceiling lights came on, bathing her in a blaze of light.

Jackie stood near the curving staircase, her eyes glittering with fear and fury. "If you knew he was coming, why didn't you stop him?"

Guilt settling heavily on her shoulders, Riya sighed. If only life were as simple as her mom thought it was. "It's his estate we're living in. One of these days, he was bound to return."

"Just when Robert has finally agreed to the wedding and—"

Unable to hear another word of her mom's self-absorption, she cut across her. "Robert will be happy to see him. I can't just send him away, even if I wanted to."

Her elegant hands wringing in front of her, Jackie walked around the huge dining table. "What does he want with you?"

"He wants the estate back."

"No," Jackie said, her tone rising, her gaze stricken. "He'll probably just kick us out if you do that. You can't—"

Even as she wished her mother would think of Riya's feelings for once, she softened her tone. Whatever her weaknesses, Jackie had found stability and peace here with Robert and the estate. "I can't stop him from taking what is rightfully his, Jackie."

Jackie's gaze zoomed somewhere far away, and Riya locked out the urge to shake her mom. That look meant nothing she said was going to get through to her now. "I don't care what you have to do. Just make sure he doesn't have the house back. Do something, anything to send him back, Riya."

"I can't take him on," Riya said, looking away. If Jackie found out he was here because of what Riya had done... "If I fight him on this, he threatened to drag us through the courts. I don't have a choice."

"Of course you can. You have Robert on your side. He'll never agree to Nathan taking the estate from you. If there's a long court battle, then so be it. You can't lose the house, Riya. I can't take this uncertainty, this kind of stress at this stage of my life."

And there was the heart of the matter. Bitterness pooled in her throat, but Riya shook it away. As she always did. "Robert will look after you, Jackie. Nothing will happen to you."

"Does it occur to you that maybe it's you I could be worried about?"

"There's no precedent for me to think that, is there?"
Jackie paled.

Now Riya felt like the green scum that lived under a rock.

Jackie sighed. "You slogged over the estate for years.

Where was Nathan when he was needed? Do whatever you have to do, but make sure you hold on to this house.

"You have just as much right to this as he. Or even more."

Nathan's dark smile as he'd stood close to her sent a shiver over her skin. His offer for Travelogue was more than she'd hoped for, but she didn't like the look in his eyes.

It wasn't just that ever-present energy between them. It was more. As if he could see through her, into the heart of her. As if he could see her fears and insecurities and found them laughable. As if he knew how to use them to trip her up.

She just had to remember that whatever he threw at her, she could cope with it. The only danger was if he had true interest in her. He didn't. Nathan was a man who traveled the world over.

Like everyone else in her life, she would matter very little to him once he realized she wouldn't budge from her goal. And then he would leave her alone.

For years, she had lived with the knowledge that her father hadn't cared about her. For Jackie, she was nothing but a crutch of safety, the one who would never leave her. For Robert, she had been the means to assuage his guilt about Nathan and his mom. Not that she didn't appreciate his kindness.

But the truth was no one had ever really cared about her, about her fears, her happiness. And Nathan would be no different.

CHAPTER FOUR

WHEN RIYA ARRIVED at work Monday morning, it was to find Nathan leaning against the redbrick building, head bent down to his tablet.

Pulling in a breath, she forced her nerves to calm down. She had agreed to this, actually forced him into this. Now she had to see this through for Robert and for her own company.

The shabby street instantly looked different, felt different. And more than one woman sent him lingering looks as they walked past. But he was unaware of the attention he was drawing.

Today, he was dressed in a V-necked gray T-shirt coupled with blue jeans that hugged his lean hips and thighs in a very nerve-racking way. His hair gleamed with wetness, his beard still hiding his mouth. The veins bulging in his forearms, the stretch of the cotton across his chest. Every time she set eyes on him, something pinged inside her.

So early in the morning, with no caffeine in her system, he was just too much testosterone to stomach.

"You're wasting my pilot's time." His gaze didn't waver from his tablet.

"Pilot? What are you talking about?" Feeling heat in her cheeks, she dug through her bag for her phone.

For the first time in two years since she and Drew had

started Travelogue, she had resolutely refused to check her work email. Now she just felt stupid because she had obviously missed some important communication.

"Not completely together still? Had to abandon the mother ship early today?"

"I need coffee before I can deal with you," she muttered. "I turned off my email client all weekend."

She had hardly finished speaking when his chauffeur appeared by her side with a coffee cup. Nathan's gaze lingered on her as she took a few much-needed sips.

His perception surprised her, but she wasn't going to confide about Jackie to him. Or anything for that matter. For all his generous offer, she didn't trust his intentions.

"I thought you slaved night and day, weekends and whatnot to build Travelogue. Didn't have a life outside of the company and the estate. Apparently you're a paragon of hard work and dedication and every other virtue. Except for the 'small incident' with Mr. Anderson."

Feeling like a lamb being led to slaughter under his watchful, almost indulgent gaze, she gulped too much on her next sip and squealed. He was instantly at her side, concern softening his mouth.

She jerked away as his palm landed on her back, scalded by his touch more than the coffee. Feeling like an irresponsible idiot, she cleared her throat. "Just…tell me what's on the agenda today."

Wicked lights glinted in his gaze. "British Virgin Islands."

Her leg dangled midway over the footpath as if she were a puppet being pulled by strings. "Like going there? Us?"

"Yes."

Alarm bells clanged in her head. "Why?"

He moved closer. She caught the instant need to step back. "A project of mine has come to the execution stages.

It'll suit very well to see what your precious team and you are made of. Sort of a test before I flush you guys."

"A trip to Virgin Islands just to test us seems like the kind of extravagance that adds a lot of overhead to small, itty-bitty companies. I would rather—"

"Didn't I tell you? Your finances, your projects—everything's on probation." Arrogance dripped from his every word, every gesture. "A skeleton crew will keep the website and sales going."

She swallowed the protest that rose to her lips. She'd have to just show him what she and her team were made of. Navigating to the calendar on her phone, she synced it and opened his shared calendar. Tilting her head up, she leveled a direct look at him. "Robert is back tonight. Should I go ahead and block your time, then?"

A mocking smile lingered on his lips as he studied her. Her breath felt tight in her chest as she willed herself to stay still under the devouring gaze. "We won't return for a few days."

"I don't see the need for—"

"I'm beginning to see why your investors were so eager to jump ship. You don't want to make money, and you don't listen to advice or input of any kind. It's almost as though you live and work in isolation."

"That's not true. I..."

Folding his hands, he raised an eyebrow.

Something about the look in his face grated on her. But she didn't want to give him a single reason to back out of their deal. "Fine. I'm ready to go."

Faced with her increasingly unignorable reaction to him, she found it tempting to just accept defeat, sign away the dratted estate and walk away. Except she had heard the stunned silence when Jackie told Robert that Nathan was here. She had heard his hopes, his pain in the one request he had made of her.

"Whatever he wants, please say yes, Riya. I want to see my son."

It was the first time Robert had ever asked anything of her.

Guiding her along with him, Nathan crossed the small, dingy street that housed their office to the opposite side. Every inch of her tautened as the muscled length of his thigh grazed hers.

"Which island are we visiting?" she said pushing her misgivings down. Robert and her company, she must keep her reasons at the center of her mind.

"Mine."

She slid into the limo and crossed her legs as he occupied the opposite seat. "You own one of the Virgin Islands?"

"Yes."

"But you don't even own a home."

Amusement deepened his gaze. "Been reading up on me?"

She shrugged, as if she hadn't devoured the internet looking for every scrap of information on him over the weekend. "There wasn't really much."

"What were you hoping to find?"

"Not the list of your assets," she said, remembering the article he had been featured in in *Forbes* about the youngest billionaires under thirty. It galled her to admit it, but the man *was* a genius investor and apparently also one of the leading philanthropists of their generation.

He donated millions to charity and causes the world over, but there hadn't been a byte about his personal life. What was she to make of him?

"I was looking for something of a personal nature."

He leveled a shocked look at her. "Why?"

"Jackie told Robert you were back and he asked me a thousand questions about you. I had nothing to tell him apart from the fact that you're a gazillionaire and an arrogant, heartless SO…"

He narrowed his eyes and Riya sighed. Antagonizing him was going to get her precisely nowhere.

"So, all this interest in my personal life is only for your precious Robert, right?"

She would jump from the thirteenth story before she admitted to him how scarily right he was. Ignoring the charged air of the luxurious interior, she went through her email. "This whole trip is just an excuse for you to—"

"Excuse for what?" he interrupted, a thread of anger in his voice. He leaned forward, his muscled forearms resting on his thighs. Gaze zeroed in on her with the focus of a laser beam. Lingered over every inch of her face until it was a caress. The decadent sides of the vehicle seemed to move inward until it was as if they were locked in a bubble.

"You're welcome at any time to sign the papers and walk away. And I'll do the same."

Shaking her head, Riya looked away, trying to break the spell he cast around them. She was nowhere near equipped to take him on. On any level.

Soon they arrived at a private airfield. A sleek Learjet with RunAway International's logo, a tangled-up R&A, was waiting. They boarded the aircraft and it was easy to keep her mouth shut, greeted by the sheer affluence and breadth of Nathaniel Ramirez's standing in the world.

The interior of the plane was all cream leather and sleek panels. Her brown trousers and ironed beige dress shirt had never looked quite so shabby as they did against the quiet elegance of her surroundings. While Nathan spoke to the pilot, she took a quick tour and came away with her head spinning.

The master suite in the back was more opulent than her bedroom at the estate.

Still reeling from the sheer breadth of Nathan's wealth, she made a quick call to Jackie and Robert, informing them of her sudden trip.

It took her a few minutes to settle down, to regain her balance that he tipped so easily. Soon they were leveling off at thousands of feet, with nothing but silence stretching in the main cabin.

"Robert asked me to tell you that he can't wait to see you," she said.

His mouth narrowed into an uncompromising line, his whole posture going from relaxed to tense in a matter of seconds. "Tell me what happened between you and Mr. Anderson."

"That's none of your…" Sighing, she tried to collect herself.

The last thing she wanted was to talk about herself and with him of all people. But if he couldn't even tolerate Robert's name, what was he going to say when he saw him? What was the point of all this if he just sat there and glared at Robert with that frosty gaze?

How hardhearted did he have to be not to wonder about Robert all these years?

If the price was that she answer questions about herself, then she would.

"There's nothing much. Drew and I shared a professional relationship. For the most part." Time for attack again. "Where did you go when you left all those years ago?"

Challenge simmered between them. If she went down this road, he was going to make her pay.

"New York City first and then I backpacked through Europe." Promptly came the next shot. "So Mr. Anderson was just a hopeful candidate you were trying on?"

"For the last time, I was not trying him on. I never even went on a date with him."

"That's not the story I've been hearing."

"I have no intention of humiliating myself or Drew just so that you can sit there and play us off against each other."

He leaned back into his seat as they leveled off, and the gray fabric stretched over his chest. "You managed it quite well all by yourself. I reviewed all of last quarter's reports, and he did nothing but run the company into the ground. With his head buried in love clouds and you averse to any risk, Travelogue would have died within a year."

Drew and she had known each other for a while, their relationship always in a strange intersection between friends and colleagues. But things had slowly spiraled to worse in the last few months. "I never expected him to sell me out to you."

"Selling out to me was the wisest thing he did. There hasn't been a lot of financial growth in the last quarter. And anyone who had good ideas, Drew fired them. Like the marketing strategist."

The sparkling water she had ordered came and she took a fortifying sip. "All the marketing strategy suggested was that we increase the cost of membership for customers who have *been* with us since the beginning, and take a bigger cut of the profits from the flash sales for vacations packages.

"These are middle-class families who come to us because we provide the best value for their buck, not international jet-setters who don't have to think twice about buying and sinking companies like a little boy buys and breaks his toys."

Nathan countered without blinking at her juvenile attack. "That marketing strategy is spot-on. Different tiers of membership is the way to go. An executive membership that charges more and provides a different kind of experience. There's a whole set of clientele that Travelogue's missing out on. If you don't grow, if you don't expand your horizons, you'll be pushed out of the market."

"That's a huge risk that might alienate us to our current clientele."

"It is. And it's one I'm willing to take."

Neatly put in place, Riya bristled. It was all her hard work and his risk. And the consequences would be hers to bear. "Does it ever get old?"

"What?"

"That high you're getting from the casual display of your power and your arrogance?"

He laughed, and the deep sound went straight to her heart, as if it were a specially designed missile targeted for her. It seemed every little gesture of his went straight to her heart or some other part of her.

Parts she shouldn't even be thinking about.

How did he get past all of her defenses so easily? Why did he affect her so much?

She had no answers, only increasing alarm that she would never figure out how to resist whatever it was that he did so easily.

"What will you do once I sign over the estate to you? Kick Robert and Jackie out?"

"Maybe. Or maybe we can all live under one roof like a happy family. Would that pacify your guilt?"

The idea of it was so absurd that Riya stared at him, taken aback.

"Horrifying prospect, isn't it? Me and you, me and your mother, me and Robert—it's a disaster every which way."

"This is all so funny and trivial to you...you don't care..." She had to pause to breathe. "You have all these resources, you own a damn plane and yet you couldn't have visited Robert once in all these years?

The cabin resounded with her outburst.

"It's not a one-for-one anymore, Riya."

He slid some papers toward her, and the words *Disciplinary Action* printed neatly on top stole the remaining breaths from Riya's lungs.

She fingered the papers, her heart sinking. "What is this?"

"His mismanagement of the company in the last few months meant Drew was the dispensable one between the two of you, for now. But it doesn't mean you're without culpability. I need to know the source of the problem between you two."

"Ammunition to make me dispensable too?"

"I'm making sure it's documented properly. It's a standard HR policy in my group of companies."

Nathan leaned back into his seat, wondering at the puzzle that Riya Mathur was. The software engine she had built, he'd been told by one of his own architects, was extraordinarily complex. And yet she blanched at using it to its full potential by expanding the client base, at spreading her wings in any way.

"This is your one chance to clear it all up," he said, softening his voice. He wasn't bending the rules, but he was also very curious about what happened between her and her colleague.

"Last year, on New Year's Eve, a week after we had signed up the half millionth member, we had a party. Drew was drunk. I...I had a glass of white wine. We...ended up next to each other when it struck twelve. He...kissed me. In front of the whole company." She looked away. But the small tremble that went through her couldn't be hidden. "I kissed him back...I think. Before I remembered to put a stop to it."

"You think? It's not rocket science."

She glared at him and pushed her hair back. "I don't know what happened or how I let it happen. Just that it was the stupidest thing I've ever done. In my defense, I had got the news that day that Robert was out of danger and with Travelogue making such a big milestone…" She ran shaking fingers over her face. "I've been kicking myself for losing control like that. I never meant to…"

"Enjoy a kiss?"

"Yes. For one thing, it was unprofessional. For another, it was reckless on so many levels. A relationship with any man is not in my plan right now. Career is my focus."

Nathan frowned, seeing embarrassment and something else. He admired her drive to succeed in her career, understood that it might leave very little time for a personal life. If not for the thread of wistfulness in her face.

Every time he had a conversation with her, he was struck sharp by how innocent she was. Yet from everything Maria had told him with grudging respect, Riya had always worked hard, pretty much taken care of herself even when she was a child. Had helped his father every way she could.

The parameters of her life—Travelogue and its current client base, the estate, his father and her mother—they were all so rigidly defined. To step out of any of them, he realized, sent her into a tailspin.

And the one kiss reflected her age, she was calling it a momentary lapse in judgment.

"You have a plan for your life?" he asked, disbelief slowly cycling into something far more insidious.

She fidgeted in her seat. "A road map, yes… Drew is too volatile, unreliable. When I'm ready to settle down in a decade or so, I want a stable man who'll stand by me for the rest of my life, who'll be a good husband and father. Right now I can't allow myself to be sidetracked by—"

Slow anger simmered to life inside him. "It seems your plan allows for everything except living."

Her gaze flew to him.

Nathan uncurled his fist, willing the unbidden anger to leave him. She was of no consequence to him. None.

What did it matter to him if the naive fool spent the rest of her life slaving over the estate and company, wasting her life instead of living it?

"Do you have a list of qualities and a timeline for when you'll meet and mate with this ideal specimen of manhood too?"

Her gaze flashed with warning. "My personal life has no bearing on you. I'm only telling you this because you're questioning my professional behavior."

"Yet you dare ask me questions about my visits, about where I've been all these years."

"That's because I've seen the pain you've caused Robert for so long. Much as I try, I can't help wondering what kind of man stays away from everything he knows for a decade, without once looking back. You didn't even stay for your mother's funeral. You didn't care about what happened to your father for a decade. You didn't come when Maria... If I hadn't realized that she knew where you were—"

"Enough."

He leveled a hard look at her and Riya knew she had crossed a line.

"I want a new software model created within three weeks for an executive membership and a package from your team on the front end. You'll see the launch event."

Her mouth fell open, her stomach dropping into a vacuum. "It can't be ready in three weeks. I'll need to redesign the whole software engine, and we don't have any of the product development team to put the package together. I have only worked behind the scenes till now."

"Then step into the front. Work smarter and learn to delegate. Use your staff as more than your cheerleader. And the next time a colleague professes undying love to you on office premises and continues to harass you, you'll immediately file a report with HR."

She slapped her palms against the table between them, something snapping in her. "How long will you hate me for what my mother did?"

"Don't overestimate your place in my life, Riya." Each word dripped with cutting incisiveness. "Although thanks to your manipulation, I'm veering toward moderate annoyance."

"Then how long will you punish me for lying?"

"Punish you?"

"Yes. Lording it over me, dragging me across the world, setting goals that ensure my failure, enforcing this…this…"

He stood up from his seat and she craned her neck.

"You've got quite the imagination for someone who's determined to live her life by a plan. We made a deal, one that you started. You're bending all out of shape now because I'm holding you to your end of it?"

His voice was soft, all the more efficient for it. The angrier she got, the calmer he grew. And perversely she wanted to ruffle that frosty, still exterior, wanted to make him angry, hurt, feel something.

That scared her more than anything.

"Or is it me personally that you can't deal with?"

She stood up, meaning to get away. "I don't know what you're talking about."

He grasped her arm, the lean breadth of his body too close. "If we're going for all-out honesty, one of us has to state it for what it is."

Panic unfurled in sharp bursts in her belly.

As long as it was unsaid, as long as it was just in her

head, and in their glances and in his knowing, arrogant smile, she could still ignore it, she could still believe it to be just a by-product of how much power he held in her life right now.

"There's nothing to state." She tugged at his fingers but his grip was relentless. Bending down, he neatly trapped her against her seat. His gaze moved over her as if it could touch her. Lingered over her eyes, her nose, her mouth. The sound of their breaths, labored and fast, surrounded her in the silence. She didn't understand where this energy was coming from or why it was so strong.

When she kissed Drew, it had been pleasant, nice. Like a breezy day on the coast, like sitting in front of a warm fire in cold winter.

When Nathan touched her, it felt as if she would come apart from the inside if he continued. Left her feeling shaken when he stopped. Probably how someone would feel when jumping off a cliff. How someone felt when playing with fire.

"Please, Nate, let me go."

A smile wreathed his mouth. It was full of satisfaction, of understanding, even a little glimmer of resignation. The pads of his fingers pressed into her skin. His breath caressed the tip of her nose, his gaze dipping to her mouth. "You didn't wonder what would happen if I came back and turned your life upside down. You didn't expect this current that comes to life when we look at each other. Do you have a plan for what to do in this twisted situation we're in?"

Emotion, that emotion she wanted to see in him, it coated every word. This unbidden fire between them, for all his forcing the matter, he didn't like or want it any more than she did.

"Do you think your life is still completely in your control?" he asked.

"It would be if you weren't so determined to play games with me."

"I haven't done one thing today that I wouldn't have even if you weren't the most beautiful, most infuriating, the strangest creature I've ever met."

A soft gasp left her mouth at the vehemence in his words. The small sound reverberated in the quiet cabin.

Releasing her, he stepped back, his gaze a wintry frost again. Glanced at her with unease. As if he didn't know what had happened.

"You are the problem, Riya. Not me. It rattles you when I come near you, when I lay a finger on you. You fight it by attributing motives to me. Tell me you'll sell the estate, and I'll have the pilot turn the plane around. Tell me you've had enough."

"Why are you fighting me so much on this?" she said, desperation spewing from her. "What do you lose by talking to Robert a few times? What do you have in there, a big hard rock for a heart?"

Her attack took him by surprise. A scornful twist to his mouth, he stared at her. And Riya could literally see the minute he decided she wasn't worth it. Whatever it was.

Perverse disappointment flooded her and she stood immobile in its wake.

"I have no heart. At least not a working one." His mouth barely moved, his jaw clenched tight. "I'll never forgive him for what he did to my mother. He let her down when she needed him. Flaunted his affair with Jackie in her face. Just the mere thought of him fills me with anger, reminds me of my own weakness."

CHAPTER FIVE

Riya straightened in her leather seat as they touched down on the runway. She had spent the entire flight alternately staring at the screen and catching sneaky glances of Nathan. He, however, seemed to have very effectively removed her from his mind.

The new software model that he had demanded loomed high at the back of her mind, but she was way too restless to focus.

As much as it galled her, the infuriating man was right.

All these years, she had drowned herself in work, focused on the estate and Robert and Jackie. Had spent it all denying herself a normal life.

What was the point in inviting anyone into her life when all she faced in the end was pain and disappointment? When, inevitably, she would be deserted? A small mistake, and look how easily Drew had walked away from her. Wasn't it better than the hurt that followed if she allowed herself to form any kind of attachment, to constantly look inside and wonder what she was lacking?

For years, she had wondered why her father had given up on her so easily, why she wasn't enough for Jackie as she struggled herself...

Safer to focus on work, to develop her career. At least, the results were dependable. But it also meant she was woefully unequipped to deal with her attraction to Nathan. And all the ensuing little things she was sharply becoming aware of.

Simple things like how different the texture and feel of his hand was against hers. How the scent of him invaded her senses when he stood so close. How there was a constant battle within her between reveling in what he evoked and fear that she was losing control.

How slowly but surely his words were beginning to affect her...

As she followed him down the plane's stairs, she stilled on the second step, taking in the vast expanse of land, a beautiful landscape of beaches and water. Her mouth slack, she blinked at the sheer magnificence of it.

The island was a paradise and apparently Nathan's next billion-dollar venture.

A team of engineers and architects greeted him, all dressed in casual shorts and T-shirts. "Is Sonia still working?" he asked, and was told yes.

Her curiosity about the island and the project he had mentioned trumping everything else, Riya stayed behind him. His attention to detail, his incisive questions...it was like watching a super computer at work.

The island, she learned, was to be rented out as a private retreat to celebrities who wanted a slice of heaven to get away to, at a staggering half a million dollars per day. The tour they had been given, driving around in buggies, had permanently stuck her jaw to her chest.

There were a hundred acres of heaven, with six Balinese-style abodes, a submarine that could be chartered to see the untouched coral reef, a Jacuzzi that could apparently house two dozen people at once and an unnamed attraction that everyone mentioned with sheer excitement. Also included on the island were private beaches, infinity pools that led into the ocean, tennis courts, a wide array of water sports and every single abode came with a personal chef, a masseuse and a housekeeping staff of ten.

No small detail was beneath Nathan's attention. He had even asked after the scientific team dedicated to studying an almost extinct gecko that was native to the island.

The more Riya saw, the more guilt and awe gripped her insides.

He owned all this and he still wanted that small estate. He had chosen to accept her little deal when he could have done anything with her company, with her and not looked back. That didn't speak of a heartless, uncaring man, and Riya struggled to accept what it did mean.

Just the mere thought of him fills me with anger, reminds me of my own weakness.

His words pinged incessantly in her head all afternoon. Beneath the cold fury, there had been so much pain, an ache that she understood. All she knew was that his mother, Anna, had died of a heart condition. But why say Robert reminded him of his own weakness?

Seeing his dynamic interactions with his team, however, his face wreathed into laughter at something, she found it hard to see any weakness in him. He was gorgeous, wealthy and possessed of an incisive mind that had made him a billionaire.

Sometime since they had arrived, he had changed into khaki shorts and a cotton T-shirt. The relentless sun caressed his face, glinted in his beard, reflecting myriad shades of blue in his eyes. The watch on his wrist glinted expensively as he signaled to someone, and his hands and arms caught her attention.

His gaze found her right then, as though he was aware of her fascination, and she dragged her own back to the delicious food that they had been served. They were lunching on the covered terrace of one of the villas.

Fresh water cascaded into a whirlpool on the terrace below and poured into the enormous swimming pool, its water as clear as crystal. The living area was cavernous with tropical sunlight streaming in from every direction.

Using local stone and Brazilian hardwood floors, the villa was an architectural beauty that boasted ten bedrooms. Decorated with priceless antiques, Indian rugs, art pieces and bamboo furniture from Bali, the villa was situated above a hill providing a spectacular view of the beach.

The chocolate soufflé had barely melted in her mouth when Nathan sat down in the chair next to her.

"What do you think?" he asked, and his entire team had come to a grinding halt as though his very question to her demanded utter silence.

Riya had met his captivating gaze, warning herself not to read so much into a simple question. "Everything is brilliant, gorgeous," she replied, feeling his scrutiny like a warm caress. "But you don't need Travelogue to find high-end customers for this place."

She had known he had dragged her along only to make her uncomfortable. Still, disappointment slashed through her. For a few hours, she had forgotten their little deal, had felt like a part of his dynamic team, had realized how much she had been missing living in her own world.

"I have something else in mind for Travelogue. The island is the place we're testing it out. Also, every year, there will be three months when we'll offer up the six villas independently for a deal. A special sale for our low-end customers, a chance for an average man to experience a little slice of heaven."

"And the income from those three months? It goes to a charity, doesn't it?"

The Anna Ramirez Foundation, she remembered, her heart feeling too big for her chest.

"Yes."

"I don't know what to say. Nathan, I—"

"You get to do the work." He cut her off on purpose. "I want you to build a new server plus a front-end package from your team that will tie this to the software model you will be designing. And we'll need—"

"Different tiers for pricing, and packages and even log-in portals for different members," she replied, a keen sense of excitement vibrating through her.

She had a feeling she had scratched not even the surface of the man he was. And yet she had judged him for not seeing Robert all these years. It scared her and excited her, like nothing else, what else she might learn about him in the coming weeks. And there was no way to turn back from this, no way to curb the curiosity that swept through her.

"Maybe you'll last long enough with me, then," he said, standing up.

Riya looked up, hanging between the urge to apologize, why she had no idea, and to leave the status quo. There was something about the tone of his voice that said he had neatly pushed her into the employee box. That he regretted the tiny little fracture in his control earlier.

The easy humor, the carefully constructed indifference, they were all a foil for something beneath, something deeper. Riya wanted to run away and delve deeper at the same time.

"Take a couple of hours off. The island heat can be too strong for newcomers."

She nodded, feeling a strange sense of disappointment as he walked away.

Nathan was e-signing a bunch of documents for his virtual manager when he heard more than one long sigh from his engineering team and a subdued curse fall from the local construction crew they had hired.

Baffled by the sudden change in the tenor, he looked up from his tablet.

His own breath fisted in his chest. Languid energy uncoiled in his belly.

Clad in a white stretchy top that hugged the globes of her lush breasts, and denim shorts that showcased the lean muscles in her long legs, Riya was coming down the steep path. Her hair was tied into a high ponytail and swung left and right with her long stride. She wore flats, the strings of which tied around her ankles in the most sensual way.

He couldn't fault his team for losing their focus, nor fault her for her simple attire. The weather was a combination of damp and stifling heat.

Every inch of him thrummed with tension and anticipation. Locking his jaw, Nathan turned away. Fought the insidious thought supplied by his mind that he could have her if he wanted.

Her skin glistened golden in the sun. And it felt like raw silk, he knew now. And her brown eyes took on the darkest shade when he touched her. The faintest whiff of roses clung to her skin. Two tiny things about her that he would never be able to erase.

Even as he warned himself, his gaze traveled over the modest neckline of the sleeveless T-shirt that draped over her lush breasts and dipped to her waist.

She stopped and looked around her with a smile that only added to her appeal.

The need to run his fingers over that graceful line of her neck, to sink his hands into her hair, to shake loose the safe, sterile world she had built for herself, to be the one to wake her up to her own potential in every way was almost overwhelming.

She was like a beautiful butterfly that refused to leave the cocoon, and he wanted to be the one to lure her out.

With a curse that punctured the stunned silence around him, he shot up from his seat. Turned away from the temptation she presented. Reminded himself that he had conquered obstacles and fears that were far more dangerous.

Things were already too twisted between them. And from her episode with Drew, he knew she could never handle him.

Nathan needed the rule-following, road-map-for-my-life female in his life the way he needed a heart attack.

What he should do was to put her on a flight home immediately and forget her or her little deal.

And yet with the excitement thrumming through her as she reached them, her wide eyes taking in the equipment around, he couldn't find it in him to break his word.

Three more months of this torture, and he was already chafing against his own rules.

Pushing her shades on to keep the orange glare away, Riya looked around herself. All the guesses she had made were off by a mile. It was not a casino, or a resort or a theater or an architectural marvel of any kind.

A huge crane stood behind the working team. An enclosure that was as tall as her surrounded the crane.

Her heart beating with a thunderous roar, she stepped inside and stilled.

A raised platform with an exquisitely designed, waist-high iron railing that went all around sat center stage in the enclosure. The most luxurious little sofa with legroom in the front sat against the back wall, and Riya noted that it was riveted to the wooden floor of the platform. As she watched with spiraling curiosity, tiny little lights, strategically placed around the perimeter of the floor turned on, casting brilliant light around.

Two small tables sat on either side of the sofa. Exotic orchids in vases along with an assortment of other things like expensive chocolate and even a bucket of champagne in ice sat on the tables.

And the final thing she noticed was safety tethers on each side of the sofa.

Her breath hitched in her throat as she realized what the elaborate setup meant.

She turned around, determined to find out if the fantastic idea was really true, when Nathan and a tall brunette stepped inside the enclosure.

Meeting her gaze, Nathan tilted his head toward the newcomer. "This is Sonia Lopez. She's the project manager."

A kind of suspended silence hung in the air where the woman obviously waited for him to say more and then gave up.

"Riya Mathur. She's the software architect on a company I acquired recently."

Relief sweeping through her, Riya shook the woman's hand.

Sonia cast another quick look toward Nathan before stepping out of the enclosure.

Leaving her alone with Nathan.

She jerked as he clasped her wrist and tugged her toward the raised platform. "Let's go."

Her eyes wide, fear beating a tattoo in her head, she shook her head. "No. I would very much like to be a spectator, thank you."

The most unholy delight dawned in his eyes, a wicked fire that turned them into a fiery blue. His mouth curved into a smile; it was the most gorgeous he had ever seemed to her. There was no facade, no frost. Only pure, undisguised laughter at her cowardice. "Not a choice. If you want—"

Surprising him, she took a few steps forward and cast a quick glance at the setup. "It's not fair, Nathan. My going on this has nothing to do with my company's abilities."

"Life's not fair, Riya. But you have to grab your thrills where you can."

With that, he pulled her and they stepped through the railing.

"You sound like a little boy going on an adult ride for the first time."

He clasped her hand and pulled her down to the sofa. Her knees quaking, she managed to stay still as he clipped the safety belt around them. And now, instead of an intangible one, there was a rope binding them together.

Breathe, Riya.

Within minutes, a faint whirring began and the crane unfolded, lifting them up into the sky.

Riya gasped and clasped his hand tighter, at the sheer magnificence of the feeling. Her mouth dry, she laughed giddily as they went higher and higher.

The whole island was laid out beneath them like a glittering jewel. The villas, the infinity pool, the beautiful grounds, she had never seen a more breathtaking sight. Her heart raced at a thunderous speed, a strange pull in her stomach.

When it felt as if she could extend her hand and touch the clouds, they came to a standstill. She found her gaze drawn to Nathan's profile.

His nostrils flaring, he looked around them, his eyes glittering with thrill and energy.

It was the most exhilarating thing she had ever been part of, the most beautiful sight she had ever seen. And the effect of it still paled against the sheer masculinity of the man holding her hand.

Panic surged within her and Riya breathed in greedy gulps. He tightened his clasp on her fingers. "You okay, Riya?"

She nodded and met his gaze. "This is your true thrill, isn't it?"

The safety belts forced them much too close for her comfort. When he turned, his thigh pressed against hers and Riya sucked in a sharp breath through a dry throat. "Yes."

Laughing, because it was just impossible not to when you were hundreds of feet in the sky, Riya nodded. "It's spectacular."

"I think so."

"I hope it's not going to be limited to this island," she said, thinking of how many people, average people like her, would miss it if it were. "Something like this, everyone should have access to it."

He turned to look at her, a warmth in his eyes. "We're aiming for Las Vegas, Paris, Bali, São Paulo, Mumbai, London in the first round. As soon as the approvals are in, we'll launch the new level of membership and also offer an exclusive offer to our low tier members at a discounted price."

Riya glanced around once again, her heart swelling in her chest. "It's going to be magnificent. What's it going to be called?"

He shrugged and smiled. And Riya felt a different kind of pull on her senses. "Haven't decided yet," he said.

Before she could blink, the safety tether loosened. Imagining them plummeting to death, Riya gasped and held on tighter.

Only to realize that Nathan had undone the belt.

"No…no…no…Nate…Please *Noooooo*," she screamed as he tugged her up until they were standing. He dragged her forward to the railing, and the whole setup swung in the air. Her stomach lurched, and Riya plastered herself to him from the side, breathing hard.

He stiffened for an infinitesimal moment even as the ridges and planes of his lean body pressed against her.

Adrenaline pumped through her, her muscles trembling with a thousand little tremors. She was shamelessly plastered against his back, but for the life of her, she couldn't seem to peel herself away from him.

His fingers tugged at her arms around him. His smile dug grooves in his cheeks. His hair was wind-ruffled; his eyes were glowing. "Don't worry, Riya," he whispered, tucking her tight against his side. "I won't let you fall."

Sandwiched snugly against his side, Riya looked around at the magnificent sight.

Her heart boomeranged against her rib cage; her senses spun. It was a moment of utter perfection, of glorious beauty.

When he pulled her back down, she went reluctantly, suddenly loath for it to be over.

Letting her breath out slowly, she settled into the moment, grateful to him for allowing her to be a part of it. They sat like that for a while. Everything about the evening cloaked them in intimacy.

Gratitude that he had given her a chance, that he'd let her be a part of this, and some unknown sensation she couldn't stem welled up inside her. And beneath it, Riya felt a sliver of fear that she was crossing into unknown territory. "Nathan, I'm very sorry for everything that…for all the hurt we caused you. I can't imagine what you must have felt learning about Jackie and me so soon after she died. I'm so—"

His arm around behind her, he turned, and his finger landed on her mouth. "I don't require an apology from you."

Raising her gaze to his, Riya forced herself to focus on

his words rather than the sensation of how her own mouth felt. "Is Maria right? All these years, would you have come back if Jackie and I had been gone?"

"No, I wouldn't have. Leave the past where it is, Riya. Come out of your cocoon, and live your life, butterfly."

The warmth in his endearment caused minute little flutters all over her.

"Just because I don't stand hundreds of feet in the sky and touch the clouds on a regular basis doesn't mean I'm not living," she countered.

His long fingers landed on her jaw, the abraded tips pressing into her skin. Their legs tangled in front of them. He shifted sideways until he was all she saw. Found herself staring into languid pools of molten hunger.

Desire punched through her, every inch of her thrumming with alarm and anticipation.

They were hanging in the sky with a slice of paradise laid out beneath them for as far as she could see. And the man in front of her, the most gorgeous, the most complex man she had ever met. In that moment, something she had held tight inside her, something she hadn't even realized existed, slowly unraveled.

Just a little movement of his head and suddenly his breath feathered over her nose.

Her fingers landed on his chest, to push him back. But the thudding roar of his heart beneath muted any rational thought. A slow fire swirled low in her belly, spreading to every inch of her.

One long finger traced her jawline in reverence, the tips of the others grazing her neck. "I think it's the most terrible thing in the world that you don't know whether you enjoyed a kiss or not, butterfly. The most horrible thing that no man has shown you, without doubt."

Liquid desire darkened the ice blue into the shade of a cloudy sky.

Every other thought faded from her mind except this man, every other sound faded except the loud peal of her own pulse. Every other sensation fled except for the insistent and answering thrum of her skin at the hunger in his eyes.

The brush of his lips against hers was at once cool and hot, testing and assured, bold and yet inviting. His beard rasped against her tender skin, wreaking havoc on her. The contrast of his soft lips and the roughness of his beard... her entire world came crashing around her.

It was her own response to the press of his soft mouth that blew her apart, the strength of the deep longing that jolted to life inside her. Her fingers crinkled against his shirt as he increased the pressure and the back of her head hit the leather.

Heat, unlike any she had ever known, slithered and pooled in every molten muscle as he licked her lower lip. His body teased against her own, a soft invitation to press herself against the hardness.

She purred, like a stroked cat, and gasped at the curl of pleasure and instantly, he pushed on. Only when it vibrated through her did she realize that it was a groan that fell from her mouth. Pleading for more, demanding more.

And it wasn't just their mouths that were touching anymore. His fingers inched into her hair and held her slanted for him; his lean body enveloped her; he was everywhere.

He felt alien, yet familiar. Her thighs trembled, locked against the tensile strength of his; her belly dipped and she groaned.

The tenor of the kiss went from slow, soft appraisal, a testing of fit and sensation to pure, exploding, ravenous heat.

He bit and stroked, nibbled and licked. He kissed her as if they would both drown if he stopped, and that's how it felt. So she let him. Stayed passive and panting under his caresses, let him steal her breath and infuse her with his own.

A freeing desperation joined the molten warmth inside her.

When he stopped, when he sucked in a shuddering breath, everything inside Riya protested that he did. She flushed as he pulled back and locked eyes with her. His gaze was the darkest she had seen yet, his breath coming in and out a little out of sync. The pad of his thumb moved over her lower lip, and she shivered again.

"Did you enjoy that kiss, butterfly?"

Riya fell back against the couch, her fingers on her still-trembling mouth.

That kiss had been beyond perfect. But the mockery in his eyes grated; the laid-back arrogance in it stung. It was nothing but a challenge to him. Whereas the entire foundation of her life had shaken.

"I would have been surprised if I hadn't," she said, dredging up the cool tone from somewhere. Her fingers still on his chest, she glared at him. Her heart still hadn't resumed its normal pace. "Very altruistic of you," she said, a little hollow in her chest, waiting for him to deny.

He grinned instead. "I haven't been called one of this generation's greatest philanthropists for no reason."

"Forgive me if being your charity case doesn't fill me with excitement."

Turning away from him, Riya sought silence. Fortunately for her, she felt them coming down again. They had just stepped out of the enclosure when they saw Sonia waiting there, her gaze stricken, her features pinched with pain.

Mortification came hard at Riya. Had the entire crew

seen them kissing? If Nathan hadn't been satisfied with proving his point and stopped, how far would she have let him go?

Next to her, Nathan turned into a block of ice, and Riya fled fast, wondering what she had stepped into. Reaching the villa, she couldn't help casting a quick look at Nathan and Sonia.

The way they stood close but not touching, the tension that emanated from them, their body language so familiar with each other—it was clear they were or had been lovers. And the pain in Sonia's eyes had been real enough.

Here was one clue to his past, an answer to the unrelenting curiosity that had been eating through her. A streak of jealousy and self-doubt held her still.

Shaking, Riya wiped her mouth with the back of her hand. If only his taste would come off so easily. But her mind rallied quickly enough.

He had stopped so easily when he was done. She was nothing but a naive, curious entertainment to a man who built castles in the sky, to the man who made billions by selling an experience.

Riya avoided Nathan over the next few days. With enough workload to challenge her and the very real threat of losing Travelogue, it was easy. Not that she had been able to get that toe-curling kiss or Sonia and her stricken expression out of her mind.

Determined to assure Sonia, and herself, that there was nothing between her and Nathan, she had gone looking for her the next evening. Only to find that Sonia had left the island that morning.

The fact that Nathan had so neatly, and quietly, dispatched her infuriated Riya. How dare he comment on her conduct when he possessed no better standards? Was this the true Nathan, flitting from woman to woman and walking away when he was done? Why did she even care?

But she kept her thoughts to herself, the very absence of his easy humor over the next few days enough of a deterrent.

He was her employer, and Robert's son.

She spent the rest of her days between work, fixing any defects for Travelogue's software, and her nights, soaking up the sultry beauty of the island. One afternoon the day before they were set to leave, she was working in one of the bedrooms in the villa she was sharing with four other female members of the crew.

The bedroom had open walls, with three-hundred-and-sixty-degree views of the island, bringing cool breezes in. Riya smiled, having finally hit on a solution to a design problem she had been trying to solve for two days.

She stood up and took a long sip of her fruity drink with a straw umbrella when Nathan appeared at the entrance. The cold drink did nothing to fan the flames that the sight of him dressed in a white cotton T-shirt that showcased his lean chest and hard midriff and tight blue jeans ignited.

Wraparound shades hid his expression, but Riya couldn't care. Her gaze glued itself to his freshly shaved angular jaw, traveled over his chin. The beard was gone, although there was already stubble again.

And the mouth it revealed sparked an instant hunger in her.

Men didn't have, *shouldn't* have mouths like his. Lush and sensual with the upper lip shaped like a perfect bow. A cushion of softness that contrasted against the roughness and hardness of the rest of him.

She had the most insane, overwhelming urge to walk up to him and press her lips to his again, to see how it would feel without the beard. She pointed her finger at him and heard the words fall from her mouth. "You shaved it."

Instant heat flared in his gaze, and Riya gasped, only then realizing she had said it out loud.

"What did you say?" he said, coming farther into the room, and she wished she could disappear.

"Nothing," she managed, lifting her gaze to his. "Were we supposed to meet?"

He looked behind her and saw the papers she had been scribbling on and her laptop. "Riya, why didn't you go with the rest of them for the submarine tour? The marine life you get to see here is unparalleled. With your record, it'll be another decade before you leave California again."

His remark grated even as she was aware that it was true. "I was stuck on a tricky design problem and I wanted to resolve it. And I did. I have an initial model ready."

The surprise flashing through his gaze went eons toward restoring her balance. "Already?" he said.

"You did put my life's work under scrutiny and up for assessment," she said sweetly, handing him her laptop.

More than once, her work had come to her rescue. From a young age, she had been comfortable around numbers and equations and then code. Because you could be sure y would come out when you put in x.

Not like people and emotions. Not like the crushing pain of abandonment and the cavern of self-doubt and longing it pushed you into. Nothing like this incessant confusion and analysis their kiss had plunged her into.

He made no reply to her comment. Took the laptop from her and sat down at the foot of the bed. After a full ten minutes, he closed her laptop and met her gaze. Shot her a couple of incisive questions. Finally he nodded. "It's better than I expected." A deafening sound whooshed in Riya's ears.

"Upload the docs into the company's cloud. I'll have my

head of IT take a look too. Travelogue can have this project based on how the rest of your team brings it together for beta testing. But, irrespective of your team, you're Run-Away material."

The whooshing turned into a roar. Exhilaration coursed through her and she damped it down. Too many questions lingered in her, and Riya couldn't untangle professional from personal ones. Only that he would always do this to her...make her wonder about things she shouldn't want. "I don't want another job. I want my company back."

He stood up and faced her, close enough to see the small nick on the underside of his jaw. The scent of his aftershave made her mouth dry. "You're halfway there, then."

"Until you remember why I'm not signing over the estate?"

"Excuse me?"

"I would like to know what you have in store for me, how far you're willing to go for..." When he waited with a grating patience, she said through gritted teeth, "You kissed me."

Nathan frowned, fighting the impulse to kiss that wide mouth again. It was bad enough that damn kiss was all he could think about. Even the incident it had instigated with Sonia hadn't been enough to temper the fire it had started in him. "And you kissed me back. I don't see your point exactly."

Something combative entered her eyes. "What happened to Sonia?"

The question instantly put him on guard. The hurt expression in Sonia's eyes had been haunting him the past few days. And the fact that he had caused her pain, even after he'd been careful not to, scoured through him.

"None of your business," he said, turning away from Riya.

Her hand on his arm stalled him. "Just answer the question, Nathan."

"You think one kiss gives you the right to take me to task?"

"No. I'm trying to understand you."

"Why?"

"You hold the fate of my company in your hand. You hold my fate in your hand. I don't think it's worth killing myself if you're unscrupulous. If you make a habit of taking your employees as lovers and then firing them when things turn sour, I'd rather cut my losses now."

"That's quite a picture you paint of me," he said, laughing at the nefarious motives Riya attributed to his actions.

Even preferred it to the truth. Because the reality of losing a friend who had known him for over a decade was all too painful, the hollow in his gut all too real. The number of people who were constants in his life over the past decade were two—Sonia and his manager, Jacob.

The realization that he was condemning his very soul to loneliness still shook him.

But then Sonia had left him with no choice, giving him an ultimatum between her love and her friendship. One time of seeking comfort with her, of breaking his rule, and she had forgotten he didn't do relationships, forgotten that he lived his life alone by choice, that he'd turned his heart into a stone painstakingly over the years.

That he couldn't let himself become weak by giving in to emotions.

He'd immediately told Sonia that it had been a mistake, that it changed nothing. That they could never repeat it.

It was his fault that he hadn't held her at arm's length like with everyone from the beginning, that she was hurt. His fault that he'd given in to temptation with the woman in front of him, even more ill-suited to handle him than Sonia.

Her fingers bunched in his shirt, Riya's brown eyes blazed with anger and confusion. "How can you be so... so careless about someone's pain? So casual about the havoc you're wreaking?"

"On her?" He gripped her hands with his, feeling a powerlessness course through him. He had punished himself by sending Sonia away, and that Riya judged him for that only fanned his fury. "Or on you and your plan? It was a damn good kiss, Riya, but don't let it distract you from your plan."

She let go of him as if he had struck her. "I know I'm nothing more than an entertaining challenge to you. And that kiss...it's nothing but you proving to me that I'm out of my element with you. But she and you have known each other for a decade, and now no one knows where she is."

He turned toward the stunning vista, his knuckles showing white against the brown of the wood paneling. "No injustice has been done to her. Sonia is a twenty percent shareholder in RunAway. She'll be all right." It was the only thing that gave him solace.

"Then why did she leave?"

"Because I told her in no uncertain terms that she has no place in my life anymore. Pity, because she was my only friend," he said in a low voice.

Riya reeled at how easily the words fell from Nathan's mouth. But the affected disinterest didn't extend to the pain in his eyes. Whatever he had done with Sonia, it hadn't left him untouched. "Why?"

"She messed up at the one thing I asked her not to do."

"What could she have done that you removed her from your life like you would delete a file?"

He smiled at her consternation, but there was no warmth in that smile. There was no mockery, there was no humor in his gaze. Only the shadow of pain, only unflinching honesty. "She fell in love with me. Despite knowing I'm allergic to the whole concept."

The impact of his words came at Riya like a bucket of ice-cold water.

"She knew I didn't want her love. She knew nothing was ever going to come out of it. But she didn't listen. Now she's cost us both a friendship that should have lasted a lifetime."

It didn't matter that it hurt him to lose that. He had still cut Sonia out of his life. He had never turned around for Robert. He was exactly the kind of man who walked away without looking back. The why of it didn't matter in front of his actions.

It was all the proof Riya needed to realize that of all the men on the planet she could have been attracted to, Nathan was the most dangerous of all.

CHAPTER SIX

FOR THREE WEEKS after they returned to San Francisco, Riya slept in one of the extra rooms that had been booked at a downtown hotel in addition to the conference room for the Travelogue team.

Nathan had given her team three weeks to put together a package for the launch event, and for her, to build the software model that would support that package. Even though he could still dismantle them if they didn't come up to scratch, he was definitely giving them a chance first.

It didn't help knowing that his own team from another company was also putting something together at the same time. He expected her company to fail and she was determined to prove him wrong.

Three weeks in which Riya had backed off from pestering him about their deal, in which she had slept only minimum hours to develop the final model for software, in which he had set a relentless pace, driving every member of Travelogue and his own team crazy. Three weeks in which Jackie had figured out somehow that Nathan was back because of Riya, that she had willingly offered to sign away the estate.

Nothing Riya said helped, not that she had a lot of time.

Nathan worked just as hard as they did, putting in long hours, giving much-needed direction and expertise. If they encountered a problem, there was nowhere to go until a solution was found.

As manic as he had been in his energy, he also had tremendous motivating capabilities. With the entire team working together in a conference hall, exchanging ideas and finding instant solutions for challenges they encountered, it had been the best workweek of her life.

There was something to his energy, to his credo of doing everything right then, of implementing an idea as best and as soon as possible.

Now the beta testing they had done of the model had been a spectacular success, and they had entered the next iteration. It was three weeks since Nate and she had struck that deal, and he had yet to see Robert.

She'd been trying to get a word with him for two days and failed. The man was a machine, traveling, working, managing teams all over the world... Knowing that tonight he was just a few floors above her, in the penthouse suite, she had to take this chance.

Squaring her shoulders, Riya took the elevator. The doors swished open and she entered the vast black-and-white-tiled foyer.

For a few seconds, she was lost in the brilliant San Francisco skyline visible through the French doors. Subdued ceiling lights cast a hushed glow over the steel and chrome interior.

She spotted Nathan in the open lounge, clad in gray sweatpants that hung precariously low on his hips, doing push-ups.

The line of his back, defined and pulling tight over stretched muscles, was the most beautiful thing she had ever seen. The copper highlights in his hair glinted and winked in the low lights.

Sweat shone over the smooth, tanned skin of his back,

his breathing punctured by his soft grunts. Warmth un-curled in Riya's belly, her own breathing becoming choppy and disjointed.

In a lithe movement that would have made a wild ani-mal proud, he shot to his feet and grabbed a bottle of water.

Her mouth dry, Riya watched as his Adam's apple bobbed. A drop of sweat poured down his neck and chest, which was lean with sharply bladed muscles. A sprinkle of copper-colored hair covered his pectorals and formed a line down his hard stomach. His shoulder bones jutted out, his throat working convulsively as he swallowed. He wasn't pumped up with bulging muscles, but what was there of him had such sculpted definition that her fingers itched to trace it.

She had the most overwhelming urge to cross the hall and to press her hands against that warm skin, breathe in the scent of him.

Shivering from a heat that speared across her skin like a fire, she was about to clear her throat when she saw him sway. He was so tall and lean that it was like seeing an im-movable thing buck against a faint breeze. Her heart lurched into her throat as his knees buckled under him.

Riya didn't know she could move so fast. Working on auto, she grabbed his shoulders just as he sank onto his haunches, his head bent. She tapped his cheek, fear twist-ing in her gut. "Nathan…Nathan…"

She ran her hands all over him, his shoulders, his neck, her throat aching. "Nate, honey? Please look at me…"

His fingers closed on her upper arm, almost bruising in their grip, and he slowly raised his head. His gaze remained unfocused for a second longer, before it rested on her face. He blinked then. "Did I scare you, butterfly?"

Fear still clawed at her, but she fought it. This was

ridiculous. He was right in front of her, solid and arrogant, as always.

"Riya?"

"Yes?"

His fingers moved from her arm to her wrist, firing neurons left and right. "Don't leave just yet, okay?"

She nodded, the stubble on his jaw scratching against her palm. He didn't look dizzy or disoriented.

Slowly he peeled her fingers from his jaw but didn't let go. "Are you all right?"

Breathing hard, Riya pulled her hand, but his grip was firm. "Me?" She licked her lips and his gaze moved to her mouth. "I'm fine. I thought you...Nathan? You almost fainted."

Something flickered in the depths of his eyes. For a second, Riya could swear it was fear. But it was replaced by warmth.

He flashed a grin that stole her breath. He dragged her hand to his chest.

Skin like rough velvet, hot as if there were a furnace under it, stretched taut over his chest. His nipple poked the base of her palm. His hand covered hers as his heart raced beneath it. "See? In perfect working condition," he murmured, but Riya had no idea what he meant.

And his gaze locked with hers again.

It lingered there with such focus that she wouldn't have known her name then. All she wanted was to sink into his touch, to make sure he was all there. He was always so incredibly focused, so unbearably driven that the seconds-long spell fractured something inside her. Something knotty and hard sat uncomfortably in her throat, and giving in, Riya threw her arms around him. Buried her face in the crook of his neck and closed her eyes. "You scared the hell out of me, Nathan."

He was like a hard, hot statue for a second, and then his hands moved over her back slowly. For a second, his arms were like vines around her, holding her so tight and hard that her lungs struggled to work, and Riya felt her armor shatter.

"Shh. I'm okay," he finally said, releasing her. Pulling her hands forward, he clasped her face with his hands, a burning resolve in his eyes. "I do, however, need a little fortification, butterfly." His breath came in little pants as he made a lithe movement and tugged at her lower lip with his teeth.

A peal of shuddering pleasure rang through Riya and she shivered all over. Gasping at the sharp nip, she braced herself against him. Had every intention of pushing him back. But the moment her palms landed on his shoulders, she was a goner.

With a ragged groan, he covered her mouth again.

He was hot, sweaty, hard, trembling and he was everything she wanted right then. His fingers crept into her hair, held her hard as he stroked her mouth, changed angles and kissed her again.

As if he couldn't stop, as if he couldn't breathe if he did, as if his entire universe was reduced to her.

At least that was how it felt to her.

He pushed her to the floor, and her limbs folded easily.

"Nathan," she whispered as he covered her body with his and claimed her mouth again. He didn't just kiss; he devoured her, ensnared her senses. He made her feel giddily excited and incredibly safe at the same time.

"Please, Riya." His tongue traced the seam of her lower lip; his fingers tightened in her hair. "Open up for me."

The guttural request sent Riya over the edge.

He teased her tongue, nibbled her mouth, bit her lower

lip and when she gasped into his mouth, he stroked it with his tongue. She couldn't breathe with the pleasure as he sucked at her tongue.

This kiss was so different from the first one. It wasn't about give or take. It was about claiming, possessing, about wringing an earthy response that she couldn't deny. It was all about what their bodies did together, how perfectly soft she was against his hardness, how a simple touch and gasp could send them both shuddering.

Her breasts became heavier; her nipples ached. Her spine arched as he locked her hard against him, every inch of him pushing and pressing against her trembling body.

Because lying underneath his shuddering body, lying underneath all the rippling muscle and heated hardness, she felt he was her universe. She opened her legs to cradle him and he moaned against her neck, ground himself into her pulsing heat with a hard grunt.

To feel the hard length of him throb against her aching core, to hear the violent curse that fell from his lips as she moved her pelvis against that unrelenting hardness…it was bliss. It was heaven. And it was nowhere near enough.

"Oh, please, Nate…" Her whisper was raw, close to begging.

She wanted to peel her clothes off, wanted to feel the rasp of his rough skin against her softness, wanted to touch the rigid shaft that was pressing against her sex.

He traced a heated path to her neck and Riya gasped, finding purchase in his shoulders. When he sucked at the crook of her neck while his hand closed over her breast, she bucked off the floor.

And hit the tiled floor with a thud. The impact vibrated through her and she gasped again, her head reeling with pain.

With a curse, Nathan pulled them both up to their knees, his fingers sinking into her hair. Her chest rising and falling, Riya stared at him, shock holding her still under his concern. She felt winded and yet every inch of her also tingled, throbbed. Deprived.

What had she done? What was happening to her? Another few minutes and she would have let him make love to her right there, on the floor. *Begged* him to finish what he had started. A shudder racked through her.

His touch gentle, Nathan clasped her jaw. "Riya, look at me."

Jerking away from his grasp, Riya rose to her feet and straightened her clothes and her hair.

He approached her and she scuttled away again toward the door.

"Stop, Riya." His brow tied into a fierce scowl. "I just want to make sure you're okay."

She shook her head, incredibly frustrated and scared and wound up. "I needed that thud," she said jerkily. "Because it's obvious I've lost all sense. You took my company, you want to take the one place that's ever been home to me, you keep kissing me and I don't stop you and now you've made me bang my head on that hard tile and it hurts like the mother of all…"

Her voice rose on the last few words until she was shouting at him.

"It does seem like you only bring pain to me, so I should be afraid. At least hate you, but why the hell do I not feel either?"

"Don't know." He sounded inordinately pleased with her unwise declaration.

She risked a look at him, saw his mobile mouth twitching and burst into laughter herself. "It's not funny," she yelled at him, even as more laughter was on the way.

She was doubling over then, both laughing and something else, everything piling up on her.

Before she could breathe again, she was in his arms again with his arms locked tight around her, him whispering, "Shh…Riya… You're in shock…"

Male heat, hard muscle, smooth skin…irresistible Nathan. But beneath all that, it felt incredibly good to be just held, to laugh with him, to be in this place that was both strangely intimate and thrilling. A thrill she had had too much of for one evening.

Extracting herself from the cocoon of his arms, she wiped her mouth on her sleeve. "Will you please cover yourself?"

Throwing a strange look at her, he pulled on a sweatshirt and she hurried toward the door.

He appeared between her and the door, his gaze concerned. "You hit your head pretty hard. Check and see if there's a bump."

"I'm fine," she said.

This was not okay; this was not good. Only three weeks in his company and she was ready to throw away all the lessons she had learned, ready to forget all the pain relationships caused, the clawing self-doubt they left.

This heat between them, it was nothing but a challenge for him. He could kiss her and shake it off after a few minutes while the very fabric of her life shook. He would tangle with her and walk away unscathed, while she would wonder and spiral into self-pity and anger. Would forever wonder why it was so easy to walk away from her.

"You're not stepping out until I'm sure you're okay. If you don't check properly, I'll have to do it. And it won't stop there if I lay a hand on you again."

When he stepped toward her, she held him off. Fighting the furious heat climbing up her neck and chest, she poked her fingers under her hair. "There's some swelling."

His pithy curse echoed around them. Riya suddenly remembered.

He had almost fainted, she was sure now. "I thought you were going to collapse. Yet you weren't even surprised. What does it mean? Are you okay? Shouldn't you be the one that should see the doctor?"

Shadows fell over his eyes instantly and Riya knew with a certainty he wasn't going to tell her the truth. Was he unwell? "I think I just overdid it with the exercise." He exhaled in a big rush, ran a hand over his jaw. "I'll be fine. Why did you come here?"

Since they had returned, they danced around each other, avoided even talking to each other without anyone around. And today was a testament to what they had both known.

Apparently even his cold treatment of Sonia wasn't enough to make her see sense.

"I heard that you were leaving for Abu Dhabi. I won't let you leave without seeing Robert."

His hands landed on his lean hips, the bones jutting out at the band of his sweatpants. The hollow planes of his muscles there were the most erotic sight she had ever seen.

"Excuse me?" he said with such exaggerated arrogance that she lifted her gaze to his.

"Yes. To remind you that it's been almost three weeks and you haven't seen Robert yet. You said—"

"Heaven help a man who tangles with you." He shook his head, resignation filling his eyes. "I'll see him tomorrow, fine? Now shut up and sit down."

Switching his cell phone, he rattled off orders for a physician and his chauffeur.

"I don't need to—"

"Doctor or me, Riya?" he challenged.

"Doctor," she said, sinking into the couch.

Even without looking at him, she was aware of his movements at the periphery of her vision. Heard the Velcro rip of his watch. What had happened to his Rolex? Frowning, she turned and saw him look at the display and note down something in a small notepad.

He wiped his face with a towel and Riya pulled her gaze away.

Not that she had missed the rippling muscles or the small birthmark he had on the inside of his biceps. Or that instead of turning her off, even being sweaty, he muddled her senses and filled her with an unbearable longing. Or that he kissed as if he could never stop. Or that he liked having utter control even as he shredded hers.

Or that she had liked it—the way he couldn't stop, the way he took control, the way he just made it hard for her to think, the way he knew exactly what would drive her wild with longing. That she had liked how good it felt to give herself over to him, body and mind, that she trusted him as she had never trusted anyone.

All of them were things she shouldn't know about him. A bunch of things she didn't want to know about herself.

She felt raw, exposed. All she wanted was to run. Far from him, far from herself.

Handing her a chilled bottle of water, he dropped to the couch, and Riya shot up from the couch. He tugged her down. Riya slinked to the edge, her breath coming in choppy bursts. Panic weaved through her.

"You and me, this can't happen, Nathan."

"You can't control everything in life, Riya. I don't want this to happen either, but I've learned the hard way that you can't have everything the way you want it."

She turned to him, desperation raising her tone. "Don't say that, don't just…accept this."

His mouth took on a rueful twist. "What do you want me to do? Wave a wand that'll make it go away? The only solution I can think of is dragging you inside and giving us both what we so desperately want. Maybe we should get it out of the way, and things will be much clearer then."

"This is probably your MO. Seduce a woman, say good-bye and walk away. And cut her out if she doesn't accept your decision. Like you did with Sonia. But I won't fall for you. You have no heart. You're the last kind of man that I should kiss, or want, or…"

Fury dawned in his eyes, turning them into blue fire. "Is it helping, then? If my being here is turning you inside out, how about you give me the blasted estate? I'll leave tonight."

"No. I can't."

"Damn it, Riya. You're not responsible for Jackie or Robert or anyone else. You were what? Twelve? Thirteen, when my mother died?"

"Robert regrets his mistakes. I know he does. He gave Jackie and me a home when we'd have been on the streets. He always had a kind word for me. He gave me shelter, security, food. He treated me like a daughter when my own father didn't bother to even ask after me in a decade."

"Where is your father?"

"How the hell should I know? He never asked about me, never checked how Jackie has been all these years. And this is after he divorced her because she was emotionally volatile. And he let her take me. He let his volatile wife have charge of his eight-year-old daughter.

"For all her weak nature, Jackie at least looked after me in her own way. That's more than I can say for—"

"She didn't do you a favor by doing that, Riya. It was her minimum responsibility. And she failed you in that. She exposed you to her fears, to the staff's hatred at the estate. Don't you see the effects of that in yourself?"

"My life is perfectly fine, thank you. And my professional one even better, thanks to you. The last few days, working with you, have been amazing. I love your energy, I love the way you do things, Nathan. And if Travelogue can—"

"As of this morning, Travelogue has an investment of ten million dollars from RunAway International. I have ordered my lawyers to put the papers together."

RunAway International Group. The brilliant boutique of his companies offering flights, vacations, adventure trips through faraway lands... And now Travelogue was a part of that prestigious group.

Her small company...it was at once the most exciting and breathtaking prospect. She had no words left.

"I'll double the figure you make now and you'll have stock options in RunAway too. I've started the headhunt for a new CEO, and we'll find one by the time I leave."

He was going to leave. That was what she had wanted; that was what she needed. That was their deal.

Then why did the prospect sit like a boulder on her chest? What had changed in a mere three weeks?

Concealing her confusion, Riya forced a smile and thanked him just as the physician knocked on the door.

All the way through him checking on her and the limo ride back to the estate, she couldn't figure out why reaching the goal she had set for herself, why impressing someone of Nathan's vision, why achieving the financial freedom she had always craved was suddenly not enough.

Whatever his behavior toward Robert, Nathan was unlike any other man she had ever met. All her rules, all her fears and insecurities, nothing stayed up when she was around him. He made her want to know him on a visceral level, made her want to abandon her own rules, made her yearn for a connection that she had denied herself for so long.

Nothing mattered with him. Not the pain of the past, not the fear for her future, only the present. And she couldn't let this continue. Already she was in too deep, lost at the thought of him leaving.

Nathan had no idea how long he stood staring at the closed door after Riya left, the silence of his suite pinging on his nerves. Everywhere he looked, he saw her now.

Laughing, smiling, arguing, kissing, moaning, gasping, glaring...even as she denied her nature, there was such an innocence and intensity to the emotions that played on her face.

He wanted her with a sharp, out-of-control need that crossed all lines. Now that he knew how she felt underneath him...

Everything inside him wanted to make her his. Ached to own her, possess her, show her how wild and good it could be between them, longed to make her admit that she felt something for him.

Why not? a voice inside taunted him.

They were both free agents. They were both adults. And she wanted him. There was no doubt about that.

No.

How could he tangle with her knowing what she wanted in life? Even if she was determined to hide from it. How could he touch her knowing that when it was time to leave, she wouldn't be able to handle it?

She hadn't recovered even now from her father's abandonment, from her mother's negligence. Even his father's acceptance and caring of her hadn't been enough to erase that ache from her eyes.

It was in the way she was hiding from life, had slaved herself over her company and the estate, the way she took responsibility for the adults who should have looked after her.

In the way she had risked his wrath and her ruin just to make Robert smile. In the way all the light had gone out of her eyes when she mentioned her father.

And yet she was loyal, she was caring and she was strong. Exactly the kind of woman who could plunge him into his darkest fear if he let her. But by the same token, how was he supposed to walk away without stealing a part of her for himself?

CHAPTER SEVEN

NATHAN PACED THE study in the home he had avoided thinking of for so many years, fighting the surge of memories that attacked him. The study had been one of his favorite rooms with huge floor-to-ceiling shelves covering two walls completely and French doors on the opposite side that opened onto the veranda.

Thick Persian rugs that had been his mother's pride covered the floor. He remembered playing with his toys on those rugs sitting at her feet.

The smell of old books and ancient leather stole through him swiftly, shaking loose things he had forgotten beneath layers of hurt and fear.

Emotions he didn't want to feel surged inside.

They had laughed here, the three of them. Spent numerous evenings in front of the fire—his father reading to him while his mother had sat in the cozy recliner with her knitting. There had been good years, he suddenly realized, years of laughter and joyful Christmases before ruined football games and hospital visits had become the norm. Before fear had become the norm, before fear had infiltrated every corner and nook.

Had it begun with his fainting and near dying at the football game? Had it begun when his mother had been gradually getting worse and worse? Or had it begun when his father had started his affair with Jackie?

Did it matter anymore?

"Hello, Nate," his father said softly, and closed the door behind him.

Even having learned all the details of his father's illness from Maria, Nathan still wasn't prepared for the shock his father's appearance dealt him. As much as he wanted to not give a damn, he found he couldn't not care, couldn't not be affected by how frail he looked.

His blue gaze seemed dulled, haunted by dark circles underneath. His frame, always lean and spare, now looked downright skinny.

Alarm reverberated through Nate.

He didn't want to feel anything for his father. Damn Riya for forcing him to this. The blasted woman was making it hard on herself and him.

"It's so good to see you, Nate. Riya's been telling me all about your ventures and how powerful and successful you are. I'm very proud of you."

Nathan could only nod. He couldn't speak. Was he as big a sap as Riya? Because one kind word from his father and he couldn't even breathe properly.

Fury, betrayal and so much more rose inside him. And that kind of emotional upheaval scared him more than the little fracture in his breathing the other night.

If he let one emotion in, they would all follow. Until all he felt would be fear.

There were too many things out of his control already. And to be in control, he had to remember things he'd rather forget, remember things that had driven him from his home, things that had driven him to live his life alone. "Let's not pretend that this is anything but the fear and regret a man faces once he sees death coming for him, Dad."

His father flinched, and this time, nothing pierced Nathan. Not even satisfaction that he had landed a shot. Tears flooded those blue eyes that were so like his own. "I'm so sorry, Nathan, that you felt you couldn't stay here after she was gone."

He couldn't bear this, this avalanche of fear and love, of need and despair that it always brought. "It was so hard to lose her like that, so hard to see my own fate reflected in her death. But to learn that you were with that woman. Can you imagine what that must have done to her?"

"I made a mistake, Nate, a ghastly one. I couldn't bear to see her wilt away. I let that fear drive me to Jackie. I was so ashamed of myself. And your mother...I instantly told her. And she forgave me, Nate."

Shock waves pounded through Nate. "I don't believe you."

He collapsed onto the settee and buried his head in his hands. There was an ache in his throat and he tried to breathe past it, but his dad's words already stole through him.

Because Jacqueline Spear was the one thing his mother hadn't been in that last year—vivacious, brimming with life, an anchor for a drowning man. He had assumed that his dad had done that to his mom. But what if it was the reverse?

What if seeing his mom lose all her will for life had driven his father to Jackie? It was still the worst kind of betrayal, but didn't Nathan know firsthand what fear could do? How it could turn someone inside out?

His dad reached him. "I don't blame you for not believing me. All these years, I have regretted so many things and the worst of it was that my cowardice drove you away. How many times I wished I had been stronger for you."

"If you were sorry, then why did you bring them here? Jackie and Riya? What was that if not an insult to Mom's memory?"

Wiping his face with a shaking hand, his father met his gaze. "What I did was abhorrent. So much that I couldn't bear to look at Jackie for years after that, much less marry her. She was my biggest mistake given form. But I couldn't do anything to hurt Riya.

"I couldn't turn away from the child who needed a proper parent, and Jackie...she was still reeling from her separation from her husband. It was fear that drove us toward each other, that made us understand each other.

"Riya made me think of what I should have been to you, gave me a chance to rectify the mistake I made."

Nathan nodded, his throat raw and aching, a ray of pure joy relieving the burden in his chest. Something good had come out of all the lies and betrayal.

Because this man who looked at him now, this man who had cared for someone else's daughter, he knew. This was the man he remembered as his father before everything had been ruined. "Is that why you gave her the estate?"

"I had no idea what had become of you. I had no way of reaching you. And when I thought I would die...I thought it a good thing that she have it.

"Riya loves this house, this estate, just like Anna did. Everything she touches blossoms. Jackie and Riya gave me a reason to live for, after I lost everything, I thought it fitting that it went to her."

Nathan shook his head, the most perverse emotion taking hold of him. He should be a bigger man, he knew that. His mother had been generous and kind. She wouldn't have minded the estate going to Riya, going to someone who loved it just as much as she had. But he couldn't just walk away, couldn't sever the last thing that had some emotional meaning to him.

Couldn't let himself become a complete island severed from anything meaningful in the world. "She can have as much money as she wants instead. The estate is mine. If she'll listen to you, ask her to stop playing games with me and sign it over."

His father frowned. "What are you talking about?"

"I asked her to sell it to me, and the condition she put in front of me was that I see you. That I remain here for two months."

"Oh." His father sank to the couch, and Nate reached him instantly.

"What is it? Are you unwell again?"

"No. I..." His father sighed, regret in his eyes. "I ended up being another person who leaned on her too much. When she told me you were back, I told her to do whatever she could to keep you here. After all this, tell me you'll stay for the wedding, Nate."

Nathan didn't want to hear the hope in his father's eyes, fought the sense of duty that he had ruthlessly pushed away all these years. His father had needed him just as much as Nathan had needed him.

But he hadn't been alone. Gratitude welled up inside Nathan for everything Riya had done for his dad.

The more he tried to do the right thing and stay away from temptation, the more entrenched she was becoming in his life.

Lifting his head, he met his dad's gaze. "I had already decided to stay for the wedding."

A smile broke out on his father's face, transforming it. Clasping Nate's hand, he pumped it with joy. "I'm so glad. Will you live in the house again? Anna would have—"

Nathan shook his head.

He wished he could say yes, wished he could let his father back into his life, wished the loneliness that ate at him abated.

The bitterness inside him had shifted today. And the estate was the one place that meant something to him. It was also the one that would forever remind him that his time was always on a countdown, remind him of how his beautiful mother had turned into a shadow because of her fear.

Because Nathan remembered that fear, remembered what his father had left unsaid, realized that he thought he could protect Nathan from the bitter memory. But beneath his anger for his father, his fury toward what Jackie represented, Nate remembered his darkest fear now.

For the last year, his mother had become but a shadow of herself. It was what had driven his father, as deplorable as his action had been. It was what had filled Nathan with increasing fear for his own life. She had willed her heart condition to leach her life away, had only dwelled on being gone, on being parted from Nathan and his dad.

And in the end, she had become a self-fulfilling prophecy. Her fear had leached any happiness, every joy from her life until death was all that had remained.

His father squeezed his shoulder, his voice a whisper. "You've achieved so much, Nate. You won't become like—"

And Nathan swallowed at the grief that rose through him. How perfectly his dad understood him without words.

Turning around, Nathan smiled at his father. "No, I won't. And that's why I can't stay."

"I'm strong enough to face anything, Nate. I would never—"

Clasping his dad's hands, Nate smiled without humor. It was Riya's face that rose in front of his eyes. "I don't know that I am."

Just as he had accepted his own limitations, Nathan

accepted this too. Riya was dangerous to him like no other woman had ever been. Already he had broken so many of his own rules; already he was much too invested in her well-being, in her life.

He couldn't risk more.

He could never care for anyone so much that the fear of being parted would pervade every waking moment. Couldn't let any woman reduce him to that.

Over the next week, Nate arrived at the estate every evening to see his father. As if determined to create new memories for Nathan, his father insisted that he was too weak to leave the estate. And Nathan found a simple joy in indulging him.

The evenings would have been perfect, the most peaceful moments he had known in a while if not for Riya.

Every evening, he found the anticipation of seeing her build inside him. Only to learn that she was out on another errand, one of hundreds apparently and gone all evening. And the couple of times every day that he dropped into the offices of Travelogue, she was nowhere to be seen either.

One evening, he had even walked through the entire grounds and the house itself wondering if she was having his dad and the servants lie to him.

How could she be always out when he was visiting?

It had taken him a week to recognize the pattern.

The woman was avoiding him, going out of her way to make sure they didn't even lay eyes on each other. He remembered the fear that had leaped into her eyes when he suggested he give them both what they wanted.

There were three weeks until the wedding, and Nathan realized, with simmering fury, that she intended to avoid him until that day.

He should have been happy with that knowledge. Riya was not equipped in any way to take him on.

But as another day fell to dusk, he found himself thinking of her more and more. He was working long hours, negotiating a deal with an Arab prince about building a travel resort in his country, and yet every once in a while, he would look up from his laptop in his penthouse and imagine her on the floor, writhing beneath him, her curves rubbing against him, her gorgeous eyes darkened with arousal, her legs clamped around his waist.

His name falling from her lips like a languid caress.

Running a hand through his hair, he slammed his laptop with a force that rattled the glass table.

Pushing away a hundred other warnings his mind yelled at him, Nathan looked at his watch. It was a quarter past noon on Saturday, one where he should be on his private jet in less than half an hour, flying to Abu Dhabi for the weekend.

A fact that Riya was aware of. Switching his cell phone on, Nate called his virtual manager and ordered him to cancel all his plans for the day.

He found her in the grounds behind the house, knee deep in mud, pruning the rosebushes in the paths leading up to the gazebo.

The white sleeveless T-shirt she wore was plastered to her body, her skin tanned and glistened. Her long hair was gathered in a high ponytail while tendrils of it stuck to her forehead.

She looked as though she belonged there.

Nathan swallowed at the sensual picture she presented. Her skin was slick with sweat, and the cotton of her shirt displayed the globes of her breasts to utter perfection.

His reaction was feral, instantaneous, all-consuming.

His mouth dried, all the blood rushing south. Never had deprivation of oxygen to his lungs felt so good. Never had the dizziness he felt just looking at her been so pleasurable before.

He cleared his throat and she looked up. A bead of sweat dripped down the long line of her throat and disappeared into her cleavage.

Nathan fisted his hands and shoved them in his pockets. He wanted to touch her, he wanted to push her down right there on the dirt, spread her out for him and cover her body with his own. He wanted to feel his heart labor to keep up as he plunged himself inside her and pushed them both over the edge.

"You've been avoiding me."

"I've been busy with the wedding preparations. Jackie's been waiting for so long for it and she's so excited that she's practically useless and of course, Robert is ecstatic that you're here. There's a lot to do."

"Then why didn't you ask for my help?"

Her movements stilled. He realized with a pang that she hadn't even considered it.

He got onto his haunches, and her gaze flew to him. "You really think hiding is the solution? Will you hide at the wedding too? Will you hide from everything that threatens to shred your damn rules? One day, you'll be a hundred years old, Riya, and you'll be alone and you'll realize you didn't live a moment of your life."

Her mouth fell open on a gasp, and the shears clattered to the ground. She looked as though he had struck at the heart of her deepest fear. Feral satisfaction filled him.

"Get out, Nathan. This estate is not yours yet. I could dangle it over your head just as you dangled the company over mine."

He laughed and inched closer, the challenge in her gaze playing with his self-control. "You're becoming reckless, butterfly."

"Maybe. Maybe I'm tired of being dictated to by you. I danced to your tunes for my company, for Robert. Now I have a new condition. Stay away from me. Or else—"

"Or else what?" he said, a fierce energy bursting into life in his veins. A hot rush of lust swamped him. "You'll be all alone at the wedding too."

"No, I won't. My plan needed modification, true. And you just happened to be the one that made me realize that. I already found someone I like very much, someone I've known a long time. I even have a date with him tonight."

He tugged her toward him until their noses were almost touching. Until the scent of her, dirt and sweat and something floral, infused his very bloodstream. "With whom?"

"Do you remember Maria's son, Jose? He's stable and nice and dependable."

Clenching his teeth, Nathan released her, awash in burning jealousy. Because that was what it was.

The very fact that the knowledge was sweeping through him with such impact should have warned him. But he didn't heed. He couldn't even see past the red haze covering his vision.

That Jose would kiss that luscious mouth, that Jose would make love to her, that Jose would have her loyalty forever because she would give it all.

"No, you went for him because you think he'll never leave you. Jose might as well be the oak tree in the estate. You're using him. But he'll realize one day that he's nothing but a security blanket for you, that the reason you actually chose him is that you think he'll never leave you. And he'll resent you for it, even hate you for it."

She fell against the dirt, a stark fear in her eyes. "I don't need advice from a man who could cut his best friend out of his life. Now, if you'll excuse me, I have a date to get ready for."

Nathan watched her walk away, his blood boiling in his veins.

He told himself that he had no interest in her. He just couldn't stand by and watch her make a colossal mistake, waste her life like this anymore. If it was up to her, she would never leave this estate, never leave her mother and Robert, never experience anything.

Everything in him wanted to fight the chain of responsibility he felt for her, shackling him.

He made a quick call to his PA and then went back toward the house, intent on finding the woman who was going to marry his father.

He'd first hated her for a decade and then avoided her for the past few weeks. But it was time to talk to Jackie, high time for someone to think of Riya.

CHAPTER EIGHT

TWO DAYS LATER, Riya was rooting through her closet searching for a beige, ankle-length dress she'd once bought in a small designer boutique in downtown San Francisco. It would do very well for the Travelogue Expansion Launch event.

She'd asked Jose if he would come with her after the longest evening of her life. It wasn't Jose's fault that she kept imagining Nathan all evening or that Nathan pervaded her every thought.

In the end, Jose had kindly and laughingly kissed her cheek. With a twinkle in his eyes, he'd told her that, as flattered as he was that she wanted something between them, there was nothing.

She heard a knock at the door and turned around.

Jackie stood at the door. Terrified was not an exaggeration to describe her expression.

Unease clamping her spine, Riya walked around the empty cardboard boxes she had brought for packing. "Jackie, what is it? Is it Robert?"

"No. Robert's fine." She straightened a couple of books on the chest of drawers, her hands shaking.

Her unease deepened. "Jackie?"

"I've been lying to you," she said in a rush, as though the

words wanted to fall away from her mouth. Her arms were locked tight against her slender frame, her words trembling.

Riya clutched the wooden footboard, anxiety filling her up. "About what?"

"About your father."

Her entire world tilting in front of her, Riya swayed. She felt as if she were falling through a bottomless abyss and would never stop. "What do you mean?"

"He didn't abandon you, Riya. Things had begun to go downhill for a couple of years already. But he and I…we tried to work it out for you. Nothing helped. We were just too different. One night, he said he was considering returning to India. I didn't know how serious he was. But I panicked. If he took you, I would lose you forever. So when he went on one of his weeklong conferences, I grabbed you and I ran.

"I'm so sorry, Riya. I never intended it to be permanent. I kept telling myself I would get in touch with him. But then I realized what I had done and I was so scared he would never let you see me again…"

Tears running over her cheeks, Jackie sank to her knees.

Riya heard the hysterical laugh that fell from her mouth like an independent entity. Hurt splintered through her, as if there were a thousand shards of glass poking her insides.

Her father hadn't given up on her. He'd never abandoned her. The biggest truth she had based her life on was a lie.

"You ruined my life, Mom. All these years, you let me think he didn't care about me."

"I'm sorry, Riya. I couldn't bear to part with you then. And every time I thought of telling you, I was so afraid you'd hate me."

Her head hurt so much, and Riya wanted to scream. "You, you, you… It's always about you. My whole life has been about you. You were afraid to be alone, so you ran.

You were afraid I would hate you, so you hid the truth from me all these years."

Jackie clutched her hands and Riya recoiled from her, everything inside her bursting at the seams.

"That's not true. I...I know you must hate me. But I did it only because I was so scared. I...please, Riya, you have to believe me."

"Get out," Riya said, her words barely a whisper. "I don't want to look at you. I don't want to hear a word you have to say."

Casting one last look at her, Jackie closed the door behind her.

Riya sank into a heap on the floor and wrapped her arms around her, every inch of her trembling. Her heart felt as if it were encased in ice. Why else couldn't she shed even a tear?

Everything she had believed about herself had been a lie. She had let the one fact that her father had given up on her permeate every aspect of her life. Had built a wall around herself so that she was never hurt like that again.

"You're a coward, Riya."

Nathan had been right. She had done nothing but hide from life all these years. He'd even been right about her desperate date with Jose. Something even Jose had realized.

Fury and shame pummeled through Riya. And she latched on to the wave of it.

She was done hiding from life.

The launch event for the expansion of Travelogue was being held in the ultra glamorous banquet hall of the luxury hotel where Nathan was staying in the penthouse suite.

He tucked his hands into his pockets and looked out over the crowd. A smile broke out on his face as the Travelogue crew stared around the luxurious hall.

The crystal chandeliers, the uniformed waiters passing out champagne, the vaulted dance floor to the right… he had wanted everything to be on par with RunAway International.

The Travelogue crew had slogged to create the new package and had surprised him and his own team with their dedication and creativity.

He shook his head as a uniformed waiter offered him champagne. Anticipation had never been his thing, but searching for Riya, he felt as if he were looking up at the snowcapped peak of a mountain.

He had set something in motion. Something that couldn't be taken back and he felt the truth of it settle like a heavy anchor in his gut.

The fact that Jackie had told Riya nothing but lies had only urged him on. She had helped Nathan see the truth, hadn't she? He didn't think he could ever forgive his father, but he, at least, understood. Now he was returning the favor.

More than once, he wondered if he was doing it for all the wrong reasons, wondered if he was being incredibly selfish again. Had even considered picking up the phone to stop what he had set in motion. But in the end, he had persisted.

No one had ever looked out for Riya. Her whole life was built on the foundation of a lie.

Running a hand through his hair, he looked at the dance floor. And felt the shock of his life jolt through him in waves.

She was moving to the music, her gaze unfocused. And she didn't look like the Riya he had come to know in the past few weeks.

He heard the soft whispers from the women around, the shocked gasps of the men, and yet he couldn't shift his gaze away from her.

The red dress, the hair, the spiky gold heels that laced around her toned calves…she screamed only one word.

Sex.

The dress was strapless. It cupped and thrust up her breasts to attention, lush and rounded. Her skin glinted under the bright lights, casting shadows of her long eyelashes on her cheekbones.

It cinched at her waist, contrasting the dip of her stomach against the curves of her breasts and hips. Ended several inches above her knees, displaying a scandalous amount of toned thigh.

The dress so scandalously short that he wondered…

And as though as a direct answer to his licentious question, she turned around and Nathan swallowed.

Too much of her back was bare, with only a strip of fabric covering her behind.

And as he watched, she laughed, threw her hands behind her and did a little thing with her shoulders.

His mouth dried up, lust slamming into him from every direction.

Her hair, all that glorious, lustrous hair was combed into a braid that rested on one breast, calling attention to the shadowed crook where her neck met her shoulder.

She wore no jewelry. Her face, usually free of makeup, was made up, and yet not in a garish way. The bloodred lipstick matched her dress perfectly, making her mouth look even more luscious.

Suddenly Nathan was incredibly hot under the collar. His erection turned stone hard as she looked around herself aimlessly, her tongue swiping over her lower lip. It seemed the butterfly had finally come out of the cocoon, and God help the male population.

She moved again, in tune to the soft music, and this

time it was a subtle move of her hips. Threw her head back and laughed.

Her hands above her, she moved in beat to the tune. Rubbed the tip of her nose against her bare arm in a sensual move that knocked the breath out of him.

Where had this woman come from? Where had she been hiding all that sensuality?

Just then, she turned her head and caught his gaze.

Across the little distance that separated them, something zinged between them. Like a juggernaut, he weaved through the crowd toward her.

Their gazes didn't break from each other. And for the first time since she'd stormed into the office that morning a few weeks ago, Nathan saw a challenge, a daring in her gaze.

He moved fast and caught her as she turned in tune to the languid jazzy beat again.

Her breasts pressed against him and he hissed out a sharp breath. Aware that she was beginning to attract unwise attention from colleagues she would have to work with for years to come, Nathan tapped her cheek and tilted it up. "Riya? Riya, look at me."

Her gaze found him instantly and he breathed out in relief. She was only mildly buzzed. He felt her mouth open in a smile against his arm.

Sinking his fingers into her hair, he tugged until her gaze settled on him. Shock, shame and finally recklessness settled into her beautiful brown eyes. Recklessness that had his blood pounding in his veins. "Hi, hotness."

Nate didn't know whether to laugh or throw her over his shoulder and carry her out. Probably both.

She was all toned muscle and soft curves to his touch. His imagination running wild, Nathan swallowed. "This public display is not you, Riya."

"Even I don't know what I'm supposed to be." She sounded sad, wistful. "Anyway, don't be a party pooper, Nathan. I want to do one thing I've never done before the buzz in my head evaporates."

His fingers around her arms, he tugged her toward him.

"Let me go. I'm having fun. For once in my life, I'm behaving the way I should."

"And what is that exactly?"

"To live for the night. And you...you're getting in the way of my fun."

This was going all wrong. It wasn't what he had intended.

Isn't it? a voice mocked him. *Isn't this what you wanted all along?*

For her to throw off the shackles she'd bound herself with? For her to be reckless and wild? For her to realize what it was to truly live? For her to embrace life and make it impossible for him to walk away without giving them both what they wanted without guilt?

Gritting his teeth, he clamped down the questions. It was too late now. For regrets or guilt.

His arm around her waist, he tugged her off the dance floor. "This isn't what you want, Riya."

Her fingers clutched the lapels of his coat. Stretching on her toes, she tilted forward until she could whisper in his ear. Her warm breath feathered over his jaw, making every muscle clench. His entire frame shook with hunger, with lust so hard that he swayed on his feet.

"Do you know what you want, Mr. Ramirez?"

She must have licked her lower lip. But the stroke of her tongue against the rim of his ear burned through him. Turned every drop of blood in him to molten desire.

Keeping his arm around her, he pushed at her chin, until she was facing him again. "I do, Riya, with a blinding clarity. And I know why it would be wrong to take what I want too."

Large, almond-shaped eyes widened. The edge in his voice hadn't gone unnoticed. She would back down now. She would retreat under that hard shell. She always did.

She didn't and Nathan felt something in him unravel.

Long, pink-tipped fingers fanned over his jaw, and their restless wandering drove Nathan crazy. With the tip of her forefinger, she traced his lower lip, sending a shiver down his spine. "You know, you have the sexiest lower lip I've ever seen on a man. The upper one is the mean one, the one that declares to the world that you're heartless. But the lower one betrays you, Nate."

Her gaze caressed him. And Nate struggled to control his own desire under it. "It shows that you're kind underneath, that you have a softer side. Why are you so bent on keeping everyone at a distance?"

Nathan felt like the lowest scum of the world. The trust in her eyes, he didn't deserve it. He didn't even deserve to stand next to her here. "Tell me what happened."

"Why am I finally living my life like a twenty-three-year-old should? Why am I having fun?"

He steered her around. "I'll take you back to the estate."

"No." She shuddered, her balance still precarious. "I don't want to see Jackie. I can't bear to be even near her," she said with such bitterness that it stopped Nathan in his tracks. "I hate her. I didn't know it was possible to hate anyone so much."

He ran his fingers over his eyes, wondering what he had started. To see her turn from a sweet, caring person to this? It was like watching a train wreck happen knowing you had instigated it.

He sighed, fought against the panic rising through him.

Panic because he could see clearly where it was headed and still it seemed he couldn't stop it.

"Riya, you're not yourself. Let me take you back to the estate."

She tugged away from him and stepped back, her mouth pouting. "Leave me here if that suits you. But I won't go back there." She reached out for the pillar and moved toward it. "I've always taken care of myself, did you know? I'm sure I can handle tonight. What's the worst that could happen? I'll fall and land on my rear. The best? I'll go home with some stranger like every other partying twenty-three-year-old over there."

And those words...they sank into Nathan like sharp claws.

The picture they painted, her bare limbs tangled up with some faceless stranger, was enough to root him to the spot.

Nathan clasped her wrist and dragged her behind him. The swish of the elevator doors, the soft ping as it began to ascend. Everything felt magnified. As if every breath was rushing up to the moment where he would have her in his suite, dressed like this, and he and his control and his good intentions in tatters.

He still made one last attempt at keeping his sanity, at doing the right thing. "As soon as I pour some coffee down your throat, I'm taking you home."

She laughed then, her hands tucked tight around her, her entire body trembling. "Home? I have no home, Nathan. That estate belongs to you. I have no one and nothing."

"Riya, it doesn't have to be this way. I understand that you're angry. I understand how it feels when someone who should take care of you betrays you...when someone you—"

"Do you? She lied to me. About my father. She practically stole me from him."

If she had cried, Nathan wouldn't have been so scared for her. But she didn't. It was as though her shock was much too deep for mere tears. "Everything I have believed about myself, everything is a lie. I thought he abandoned me. I thought he didn't love me. I will never forgive her for this. She stole my childhood and she made me into this frozen coward who hid from everything in life. No one has ever cared about my happiness.

"Not her and definitely not my dad. If he had, knowing how emotionally weak she is, would he have threatened her that he would take me from her?"

What the hell had he started?

He had never meant to hurt her. He had never meant to make her feel alone, had never meant to unravel her like this. He understood the weight of it, he knew better than anyone how painful, how awful it felt.

"Shh, Riya. Enough," he said in a stern voice. "Look at me, butterfly."

When she raised her gaze to him, the depth of feeling that filled him scared the life out of him. Her mouth trembled and he jerked his hand back, the urge to touch that soft cushion overwhelming him. "This will pass, Riya. Believe me, let me drive you back to the estate and—"

"Please don't send me away, Nathan. Tomorrow, I'll be back to myself again. Tomorrow, I'll be strong again. Tomorrow, I might even forgive her. Tonight, I want to be selfish. Tonight, I want it to be just about me."

What could he say to that?

His chest was tight with guilt. All she had tried was to make his father smile. And he…he had unleashed nothing but hurt on her.

Because he had coveted something he could never have.

CHAPTER NINE

TIGHTENING HER ARMS around his neck, Riya nudged closer to Nathan, the warmth of his body a cocoon she didn't want to leave. As though sensing her reluctance, he didn't put her down. Not when he lingered outside the sitting area, not when he walked through it into the bedroom.

Finally he sank down in the armchair and settled her in his lap.

How had she never learned how good it felt to be held like this, to be cherished as if she was precious? How many more things had she missed tucked away in her own world?

She had erected a fence around her heart, around herself, and she had missed out on so many things. While other girls had been going on first dates and experiencing first kisses, she had been studying for a place at the university, giving Robert a hand when she could, managing her mother's moods.

She had bound herself so tight that a little truth from the past had splintered through her. Nothing had really changed. And yet everything had.

It felt as if someone had stuck a pin in her side to jolt her awake from a slumbering state. She sucked in a breath and opened her eyes. His gaze clashed with hers, his long fingers splayed out over her bare arm.

An infinitesimal tension spun into life around them.

His other hand tipped her chin up. "Why this dress? Why drinking? Why this route to show your anger, your hurt?"

And just like that, he shot straight to the heart of the matter. "I don't remember when I had decided that no man would ever hurt me like my father's abandonment did, when I decided I would live my life in this frozen state. I wanted to prove to myself that she didn't ruin me forever with her lies."

"And?"

She tucked her head into his shoulder and sighed. "It's not that simple, is it? A lifetime of sticking to the safe side, suppressing any small urge that could be deemed unsafe, that could risk pain, it's a hard habit to shake." She gave a laugh, tinged with sadness. "I was dancing and I had a little to drink, but I realized it wasn't that simple to change myself inside. Like flipping on a switch. I can't suddenly do something I've trained myself not to do."

"No, it's not simple." There was a roughness to his voice, an edge, a desperate sense of being tightly leashed. As if he was forcing himself to laugh instead of...something else.

Her hand clasped in his. Long fingers with blunt nails and hers, slender and pink tipped, coiled around his.

"It takes years to defeat that kind of conditioning, years to conquer that fear. Doesn't take much to trigger it back either." He sounded strained, almost resigned. He squeezed her arm and Riya caught the sigh that rose to her lips.

How did he understand her so well?

"How about you start with small steps, butterfly?"

She smiled and nodded, the scent of his cologne drifting over her. And the huge chasm that she couldn't cross toward living her life suddenly didn't feel so daunting.

In the shifting confusion of her own emotions and thoughts, he was constant, her awareness of him sharp and unwavering.

Nathan, who had brought so much upheaval into her life, felt like an anchor. All he lived for was the thrill, the fun, the moment. Who better to show her what she'd been missing? Who better to show her what it meant to be daring, to be wild, to grab life by the horns and shake it? Who better to start on her path to living than a man who would never affect her in any other way?

With Nathan, there would be no expectations, no disappointments. When it was time to leave, he would, and this fact had nothing to do with her. Therein lay her safety net.

A sharp hunger bursting inside her, Riya slid her fingers toward the nape of his neck. Pressed her mouth to the pulse flickering on his throat. "Is a kiss a small enough step, Nate?"

Instantly he stiffened beneath her. His fingers landed on her jaw, pushed her face away from his neck in a gentle but firm grip. Desire was a relentless peal in her, as if her pulse had moved just from some points to all over her body.

Fear and safety were taboo. Daring and living were her words of the moment.

She clasped his wrist with her hand and laid kisses against the inside of it. His palm was rough and warm, and as she pressed her lips again to the center of it, she felt the rightness of it.

"Tonight's going to be your lucky night," she said, her throat working to get the words out. She had to brazen it out, didn't want him to know how huge this was for her.

A sharp grip at the nape of her neck caused her to look at him. "My lucky night?" he said.

He looked as if his face were carved from pure stone, his blue eyes molten with desire. There was no frost, no ice tonight.

Nathan was all fire and passion, and she wanted that fire;

she wanted to lose herself in him. "Don't make promises you might not be able to keep, butterfly."

Straightening in his lap, she pushed into his touch, determined to have this. "It's okay if you're not up to it, Nate. No one wants to be a pity f—"

His fingers tightened their grip in her hair. His breath landed on her mouth, until there was nothing to do but breathe the same air as him. "You're doing this for the wrong reasons, Riya."

Feeling gloriously alive, she bent and kissed a spot just beside his mouth. The bristle on his jaw rubbed against her mouth. Heat spread everywhere, incinerating a need she had never known. So she did it again. And again. Like a cat rubbing herself against her favorite surface. Until her lips, her cheeks, her chin stung in the most delicious way, scraping against the roughness of his jaw. Until he made a feral sound that in turn scraped against her very senses.

And her desire went from a risk, a dare, to need for him. Only for Nathan.

Finally her mouth landed at the corner of his luscious mouth. And she spoke the words against his lips, felt a shudder vibrate in his lean frame. Reveled that she could do this to him.

He was like a fortress of leashed desire around her.

"I'm doing this for the only reason that it should be done for."

"And that is?" he whispered back against her mouth, and Riya ached. Ached to feel that mouth everywhere, ached to lose herself.

"That it feels so good, Nate." She moved, to get closer to him, and felt the hard evidence of his arousal against her thigh. "From the minute you stepped into my life, this… it's like a fever." She pulled his hand and pressed it to her chest. "And in all the lies and confusion, this is the one thing that's unwavering. Make love to me, Nate. I want to do all the things that I told myself I didn't feel."

She didn't wait for him to deny her. She just jumped off the ledge, hoping he would catch her. Kissed him with everything she had in her.

When her lush mouth touched his, it was all Nathan could do to pull in a breath. There was no hesitation, no doubt in the way she pressed little kisses over the edge of his lips, over his chin, over his lips, her breath coming in little pants all around him, her scent filling his nose, her fingers scraping against his scalp, holding him in place for her pleasure.

No one had ever quite so thoroughly seduced him. No one had even come close.

She was an explosion. She was a revelation. And under her honest, raw hunger he came undone. No amount of honor could compete with the liquid longing coursing through him, could puncture the desire to return her kiss, to give her what she wanted. And to allow himself what he had been craving.

When she stroked his lower lip with her tongue, tentative but still powerfully maddening, he was done being a passive participant.

Clasping her jaw, he sucked her lower lip with his teeth and she shuddered. Gasped into his mouth.

And they were sucking, nipping, their teeth scraping, their tongues licking with a searing hunger that brought the world down to only them. Pasts and futures were forgotten, only the present mattered.

Panting, he moved away from the temptation of her mouth. Sank his hands into her hair and tugged at the lustrous locks until she was looking at him.

Golden skin flushed, pink mouth swollen, beautiful brown eyes dazed with desire and daring, she looked at him without blinking, without hiding. Pushed into his touch. She was inexperienced; her kisses told him as much. But the sensuality of the woman, the way she responded, so hot and fiery. This was a battle he'd already lost.

But this was a defeat he welcomed.

When she thought of him, he wanted her to do so with a smile and a sigh of pleasure.

He leaned forward and dug his teeth into her lower lip. A gasp fell from her mouth and he blew softly over the trembling lip. "This means nothing to me except that I want you with a madness that knows no reason." He could leave no doubt in her mind. And if she wanted to stop, he was going to head straight for a cold shower. But he couldn't take a chance on risking her emotions. "I'll leave when it's time, *butterfly*. And if you want to stop this, do it now. We'll forget about it. You can take the bed and I'll take the couch."

Her gaze flickered to him, a shadow in it. And then she smiled. Her gorgeous, perfect, dazzling smile. "Falling in love, risking my emotions, it's never going to be easy for me. And with you…I could never fall for you. We're really the worst kind of person for each other, aren't we? But that's what makes this easy, that makes one night with you everything I want it to be."

Her honesty stung him, but he slashed the feeling away.

One night to satisfy this craving, desperate need for each other. That was all they could afford of each other.

Pulling her arm to his mouth, he kissed her wrist, licked the vein flickering there. Kissed a path upward, all the glorious skin warm to his touch.

Her soft tremble, her gasp as he reached the crook of her neck swept him away hard. "Shall I shock you and tell you all the different ways I've imagined having you?"

He licked the pulse there, sucked on her skin. She shivered, sank her hands into his hair. Shuddered, writhed, but he didn't let go. He continued until she was panting, moving restlessly in his arms, rubbing her breasts against his chest. He was rock hard, her volatile response tightening his own need, fraying his control.

He fisted his hands, fighting the urge to push her dress up, to drag her on top of him and thrust up into her wet heat.

Sweat beaded on his brow. And that couldn't be borne. He would enjoy this; he would drown himself in the scent of her, but his control couldn't falter.

It was all about release, all about his body. As long as he kept it to that, as long as he didn't think about what this might have meant to her, to him in a different world, beyond tonight, it was good.

Laughing, she tugged her hair away from her shoulder and looked down at herself. A blush spread upward from her neck as she ran a pink-tipped finger over the blemish. A soft pant fell from her mouth, and it was the most erotic sound he'd ever heard.

There was innocence in it and there was a raw hunger in it. For more. He had been right. She had repressed so many things, and that flicker of undisguised hunger now, of playful curiosity, turned him inside out.

Her gaze moved to his mouth and stayed there. "It stings."

Picking her up, he mumbled his apology into her mouth.

She kissed him with a searing hunger that rocked through him. Scraped her teeth against his mouth. Stroked it with her tongue when he groaned.

"Only in the best way," she whispered when he let her breathe. "I want more."

Laying her down on the huge bed, Nathan shucked his jacket and loosened his tie.

Raising an eyebrow, he let his gaze travel all over her. "Unzip, Riya."

Coming to a kneeling position, she reached for the zipper on her dress. Her fingers trembled around it. But she slowly tugged it down.

His mouth dried as the dress came loose around her chest. He was dying to see those lush breasts, those long legs, every inch of her. Just as the fabric flapped down, she held it to herself, her cheeks flushing. "Can we turn off the light, Nathan?"

"Nope," he said so loudly that she smiled. "Those prim dress shirts and trousers have been driving me mad." When she still hesitated, he stilled his hand on his shirt. "You can't see me either, then."

Something flickered in her gaze. Lifting her chin, she straightened to her knees and pulled her dress down. Over her chest, over her midriff. Leaned back onto her elbows and kicked it from around her feet.

Nathan felt his heart pump harder and harder, and for once, something else took precedence over the malfunctioning organ. His breath balled in his throat.

Her slender shoulders bare, her lush, rounded breasts thrust upward, the shadow of her brown nipples visible through her strapless bra, the concave dip and rise of her stomach, the flare of her hips, the V between her thighs hinting at dark curls...

If his heart stopped right then, Nathan would have had no fear, no regrets.

And the lack of fear, the lack of any other emotion except his feral hunger to possess the woman in front of him, was a sensation he reveled in.

Because it made him feel alive as nothing else could.

Riya had never understood what the fuss was about sex, how it drove people to the most unwise decisions.

Until now.

She'd never understood how completely it unraveled you, this desire, how completely it exposed every part of a person, how it connected one so deeply with another.

They hadn't even undressed completely, but the look in Nathan's eyes—so demanding and all-consuming, the possessive challenge that lingered there—would have sent her running to the hills.

He would demand complete surrender, of her body, her mind, even her very soul. And beneath the flicker of fear, there was also a freedom in giving herself over.

The soft fabric of her bra chafed against her nipples and her thong, which had been a necessary evil for this dress, suddenly felt intrusive, making her sharply aware of the ache between her legs, the incessant peal of need there every time his gaze traveled over her.

She was wet there and she was hot all over, and together, the sensation continued to build.

His gaze never leaving her, Nathan unbuttoned his white dress shirt, pushed it off.

All that bronzed, glinting skin, the whorls of copper chest hair, the black string hanging with a pendant over his pectoral muscles, the jut of his shoulders, the flat male nipples so unlike her own, the washboard plane of his stomach, the line of hair that went down below his navel. He was so utterly male.

And all of it was hers tonight to do with as she wished.

With sure movements, he unzipped his trousers and kicked them away. Then his boxers.

Riya licked her lips at the sight of him completely naked. Her heart thudded incessantly, her sex pulsing.

His guttural groan surrounded them, and she raised her gaze to him.

He moved closer, in touching distance. Riya raised her

hand, eager to touch that hardness, eager to learn everything about him. "You won't touch me, is that clear?"

Frowning, she tilted her head up. "Why not?"

He didn't answer.

Pushing her back against the bed, he climbed into the bed and on top of her in such a predatory, masculine way that all of her possessive claims, all of her risky resolve fled.

Leaving nothing but gloriously alive sensations toppling against her, drowning her, demanding her utter enslavement.

He was heavy over her, he was hard against her, he was hot all over and he didn't let her move. His arms cradled her upper body, raising her to him, locking her so tight against him. She was aching to touch him, dying to feel his muscles harden under her fingers...

But he locked her, leaving her no escape but to feel every assault of his fingers, his mouth, his tongue, his breath.

He kissed her until there was no breath left in her. He played with her hair...

Her toes curled into the sheets as he dragged his open mouth down her neck and to the valley between her breasts.

Need knotted at her nipples as he cupped her breasts reverently, kneaded them, lifted them to his mouth. She bit her lip, scrunched the silky sheets with her fingers, bucked against his grip. "Nate, please let me touch you, let me move or—"

"No."

"What do you mean no?" she cried.

He rose above her like a dark god, intent on pulling her under, every inch of his face carved from stone. His icy blue eyes wide, he was panting too. And Riya realized what tremendous control he was exercising, how tightly reined in his desire was. How, even being in the moment, he wasn't truly with her.

But before the thought could take root, he licked her nipple and she lost all coherence again.

"Do you want me to stop, butterfly?" he whispered hotly against her breast, his tongue laving the skin around her eager nipple.

"No," she said so loudly that the word reverberated in the silence.

His fingers tweaked her other breast, pulled at her nipple, while his mouth closed over the first one. Riya kicked her legs against the bed, and still he didn't let her move.

She gasped under the attack, she sobbed, she twisted and turned as he suckled, laved with his tongue. And a frantic pulsing began at her sex.

"I wondered," he whispered against the valley between her breasts, taking a shuddering, reverent breath.

All she could manage between catching her breaths was to say "What?"

"Your nipples," he said, rolling off her and lying on his side. His muscular leg covered her legs, his arm holding her tight against him. He dipped his mouth and suckled the swollen tip again and she arched her spine as sensations rippled and splintered through her.

The heat built intolerably between her legs and she rubbed her thighs restlessly.

His large hands stole between them, denying the friction she needed, and Riya was ready to beg. "I wondered what color they would be." This against the underside of her breasts.

"I guessed it right." This against the planes of her stomach. "Like chocolate."

He looked up then, and Riya looked down, her skin slick with sweat. She saw his gaze move over her face, her mouth and her breasts again, and felt a shyness come over her.

This was so intimate, intrusively so.

This moment when something else arced beneath the simmering chemistry between them was everything she had avoided her entire life. Here, lying naked below him, all of her exposed to his eyes, was the biggest risk she had ever taken.

For a startling second, she wondered what she had started. Wondered how she would face him tomorrow, how she would...

Moving up, he devoured her mouth in a kiss that left no breath in her. Pressed another one at her temple. "You okay, butterfly?"

Riya nodded, not at all surprised at how easily he read her. She had never met anyone who had understood her so well. Grabbing his forearm, she pressed a kiss to his biceps, flicked her tongue over the birthmark that had fascinated her so.

"You're still thinking. And I won't tolerate that, Riya," he said, traveling down her body again, trailing wet heat over her skin. His mouth hovered over the waistband of her thong, his teeth dragging against her skin. His breath sounded harsh. "You're driving me insane and I very much want to do the same to you," he said, sounding almost angry.

She could do nothing but sink her fingers into his hair.

Moan loudly as he tugged the string of her thong tight against her clitoris. And pulled it, up and down.

She bucked off the bed as his fingers explored.

Jerked as he learned her with clever, lingering strokes.

Dug her nails into his shoulders as he tweaked the spot aching for his touch. Dragged her nails over his back as he eased a finger and then two into her wet heat.

The softness of her sex felt amplified around the intrusive weight of his fingers. Every inch of her contracted and pulsed at that spot, and Riya sobbed.

"Nathan!" she said, the invasion of his fingers, the relentless rub of the pad of his thumb, the building pressure, driving her out of her own skin.

She laughed or cried, she didn't know which, her body, her heart careening out of control.

"Look at you!" His hot mouth pressed against her midriff, and her muscles clenched. "You're the wildest thing I've ever seen."

He moved his head between her thighs. The stroke of his tongue against the tight bud was like touching a spark to a building storm. "Let go, butterfly," he said, and without warning, sucked at the slick bundle of nerves.

Screaming and thrashing, Riya shattered around his fingers in a dizzying whirl of such exquisite sensations that she thought she would fall apart. Sobbing, she tried to bring her knees together, but with his fingers still inside her, he clasped her against him. Continued the relentless pressure of his fingers so that the small tremors continued until she was nothing but a mass of sensation and pleasure.

As the tremors slowed down, she opened her eyes, saw the stark need, the possessive pride written in his face. He'd watched her explode and liked it. Took her mouth in a possessive kiss that knocked the remaining breath out of her lungs. "You're a screamer, Riya…"

Fighting the shyness that he had witnessed it with such blatant thoroughness, Riya pressed her mouth to his chest. If she stopped to think, she would stop altogether.

And she didn't want to stop. She wanted all of him.

She moved her fingers down his hard stomach and down farther. Clasped the hard length of him. Flicked the soft head with her thumb, heard the guttural groan that fell from his mouth. His chest was hollow with his breath held.

The most powerful feeling exploded inside Riya. He was

so hard in her palm, and he was big. She felt the sharp need begin in her all over again as she stroked him.

He moaned so loud that she did it harder.

He jerked his hips into her hands, and whispered the filthiest words she had ever heard. Gasping at the renewed urgency in her own body, she moved her fist up and down.

He dug his teeth into her shoulder and she gripped him harder, going hot all over. Sweat beaded his skin, every muscle so tight that she wondered if he would break into a thousand shards.

Moving down, she kissed her way down his body, licking, tasting, reveling in the shudders that racked through him. When she reached his shaft, his fingers tightened in her hair, staying her. Looking up, she jerked her head. "Let go, Nathan."

His eyes were the darkest she had seen yet, his nostrils flaring, his control nearly shredded. "Tonight's about you, Riya."

"No, tonight's about what I want to do," she said boldly. Leaving him no choice, she licked down the long, hard length of him. He cursed.

She closed her mouth over him and sucked experimentally, a wet heat gathering at her own sex. She felt no shame, no shyness, only the gloriously alive feeling coursed through her. Licking the tip, she looked up at him.

And before she could blink, she was on her back and he was lodged between her thighs. "Enough," he said with such vehemence that Riya stared at him.

She watched increasingly boldly as he sheathed himself. She hadn't even given thought to protection. Coloring, she pushed up and kissed the hollow beneath his pectoral, tasted the salt of his skin, breathed in his musky scent.

The head of his shaft rubbed against her entrance. Feeling restless again, Riya met his gaze and held it, wanting all of him in that moment.

He pushed slowly at first, letting her accommodate to his length. Long fingers left deep grooves on her hips, holding her still, the way he wanted her. Kissing her mouth again, he dragged her closer, tilted her hips so she was right for him. And then swept in with one hard thrust.

Her head thrown back, Riya gasped at the sharp sting and the heavy intrusion, every inch of her stiffening. Her hands clasped his shoulders, the bones protruding out of them pressing against her palms.

His head went back in a recoil, the corded length of his neck stiff. Thick veins pulsed in his neck, his face clenched tight in satisfaction. His gaze was unfocused; then he blinked, as though fighting for control. In that moment, he looked savage, like a roaring volcano of emotions and needs, the hard shell he encased himself in falling away by the heat between them.

"Riya, you'll be the death of me," he said in such a grave tone that her focus shifted from the already receding pain.

But instead of being scared, Riya felt like a victor. Because this Nathan who wore his needs and passions in his eyes was the true Nathan.

Hiding his face in her neck, Nathan breathed hard. "You're a virgin." Of course she was. *Damn, damn, damn.*

He heard the accusatory, sinking tone of his words, but for the life of him, couldn't do anything about it.

Couldn't think about anything except the need surging through him, demanding release. She was like a fist around him, smooth and tight, and he was going to burst at the seams if he didn't move. For a man who abhorred having sex merely for the release it provided, this need to plunge into her until she was all he felt…he was drowning in it.

What had he done?

He was truly gone if it had taken him until now for that little fact to filter though.

Somehow he found an ounce of his shredded self-control, and raised his head.

Her pinched look slowly fading, Riya looked up at him. Beads of sweat glistened over her upper lip, and he fisted his hands to stop touching her.

"Do you want me to stop? You should have warned me, slowed me—"

"Would you have done it differently if I had?" the minx demanded. She sounded husky, a ragged edge to her words that seared him. "Would it have stung less? Was there a pain-free way of deflowering that you would have employed?"

Damn it, he had no wish to hurt her. In any way. "No."

This was getting too complicated. He was breaking each and every one of his rules with her. "But I would have resisted you better." *Lies, all lies.*

He saw the hurt in her eyes before she hid it away. "Then I'm glad I didn't."

"Damn it, Riya, this is not what—"

"It's just my hymen, Nate, not my heart. Except it played the gatekeeper to my heart until now."

"If you waited this long, it means you wanted it to be special."

"I waited this long because I was like Sleeping Beauty, except I wasn't sleeping but just functioning. Isn't it better I'm doing it with someone I know than a stranger? With someone I trust?

"You're my best bet, Nate. And I took it. Now it's up to you to make sure I made a good one."

She wiggled her hips experimentally, and Nathan felt

the walls of her tight sex grip him harder, the slow rub of friction driving him out of his own skin.

"Please, Nate. I swear, I won't fall in love with you. Do something. I want—"

He licked her already swollen lower lip, the pleading tone of her words sending him over the edge.

She ran her palms over his thighs and sighed. His thighs turned into hard stones. Wiggled again.

"Stop doing that."

This time, she rotated her hips, and his hips responded of their own accord. He pulled out and thrust into her. Pleasure spiraled up and down his spine. He cursed again. "How do you know how to do that?"

She smiled and winked at him, arched her spine, thrusting those beautiful breasts up, and Nathan felt himself move another inch.

Nothing was in his control anymore, not the situation, not his body and not his heart.

Her fingers moved to his hips, and she scooted closer and sighed. The rasp of it grated against his skin. The blunt tips of her nails dug into his buttocks as though she couldn't wait to be as close as possible. "I think I'm going to be a natural at this. How stupid that I waited this long... ah..."

And that broke the last thread of his control. Grabbing the rounded cheeks of her rump, he tilted her hips up, pulled all the way out and thrust back in. Slow, but letting her feel him every inch. And again. And again.

Until he thought he would die from the pleasure building in his veins, until she was sobbing his name again. But she didn't look away, didn't let him look away, and Nate wondered who was in charge, who was in control, even though he was the one who set the rhythm.

His heart pounded, raced as sensation built and clawed up his spine.

And he wanted her with him. He wanted her as unraveled as she was making him. On the last thrust in, he bent and dragged his teeth on her nipple and she exploded.

As she climaxed around him, Nathan pumped into her heat. And the tremors in her sex pushed him over. His own climax thundered toward him, splintering him into a million shards of pleasure and sensation. And nothing else.

He felt as though he was done for. His heart rushed in his ears, and he smiled, in defiance.

Take that, you useless organ, he challenged it. *Stop this moment and it would all still be worth it.*

Riya was still trembling beneath him, he realized, and he was crushing her with his weight. He meant to move off her, but her fingers clenched around his biceps, holding him still.

"I'm too heavy for you. Let me go."

She hid her face in his chest, and his muscles clenched under her tender kiss. "I can breathe. Just a minute... Please, Nate."

For a few minutes, which actually felt like an eternity, Nate cradled her face in his hands. Rubbed his lips against hers, heard the thundering roar of her heart and her breaths trying to keep up with his.

Lingered in the moment until his heart swelled in his chest.

And slowly, as the haze of the pleasure faded, as his breathing resumed normality, regret and remorse rushed in.

He felt her kiss his forehead, wrap her arms around his shoulders.

Found his own arms moving to wrap around her, to hold

her close, to tell her how explosive it had been. To tell her that sex had never been this personal for him.

"Nate?"

The whisper of his name at his ears was an intimacy that had him hardening inside her again. "Hmm?"

"Is it always like that?"

No, it wasn't always like that. In fact, it had never been like that for him.

Looking into her eyes, he said in a matter-of-fact tone, "With the right partner, it could be."

Her palms traced the ridges of his back. "Oh."

He pushed a lock of hair that fell forward. "And you were right. You're quite the natural at it. You're explosively responsive and any man would…"

The very idea of Riya with another man made him sick to his stomach.

Sudden panic surging up within him, he jerked away from her. Rose from the bed and walked into the bathroom without looking back. Turned the shower on and stood under it.

He never indulged in the intimacy of holding his lover or sleeping with one in his bed. He had never wanted to, if he were honest. In that first year after he left home, all he had done was take, as if the whole world were for his own personal enjoyment, everything in it his prize.

And waking up tangled with a woman whose name he didn't know and would never know, in an unending cycle of seeking comfort and escape from his fate and fears, bitterness had risen in his mouth one day.

Until he'd realized that at the end of all of it, the truth had never changed.

It hadn't made him stronger or smarter or healthier. It had only made him disgusted with himself. And he had realized that even this total loss of control, this gorging on things, was also driven by fear. So instead he'd put rules in place for himself.

Never get involved. Ever. Sex, even as he hated the casual, transient nature of it, had to remain impersonal.

Traveling as he did, working as he did, he'd found it easier to keep to his tenet. He had never had a girlfriend; he had never had a first date or a second date. He'd never taken a woman to dinner, never gotten to know one.

He had never even hugged one or comforted one as he had done tonight. Never let a few minutes of his life be about anyone but himself. Never let anyone get under his skin.

And now everything inside him roared with a savage intensity, raged against an unknown fate. He pummeled his hands against the tiles, bent his head in defeat as the water pounded over him.

A longing like he'd never known burst free inside, spreading through him like an unstoppable virus, and he shivered under the hot spray.

Because he wanted to go back into that bedroom.

He wanted to hold her, kiss her, he wanted to tell her that what they had shared was special. Even his untried heart knew that. He wanted to tell her that he was glad that she'd trusted him for her first time, that for all the hurt she had lived through, there was an intrinsic purity and courage to her emotions.

He wanted to tell her that the thought of her sharing her body with anyone else lanced him like a hot poker, that the thought of her sharing her emotions, her fears and her joys with someone else filled him with a hot fury.

But if he did, he would only make it harder on both of them. Make it awkward for the rest of his stay. Would push her into making more out of it.

He'd never let anyone close in his entire life. And he didn't intend to start now.

Even if she was the most extraordinary woman he had ever met.

He was gone.

Riya opened her eyes and felt the silence around her, touched the empty silk sheets and closed her eyes again. Locked away the sting of his withdrawal. Pulled the sheets up to her neck and scrunched tight into herself.

She ran the tip of her finger against her lips and found them swollen. Her arms trembled, her thighs felt as if she had run a marathon. Her body throbbed and ached after his deep thrusts. Even her scalp tingled, an aftereffect of how tightly Nathan had held her when he climaxed. Her hips bore the evidence of his loss of control, of his passion— pink grooves where his fingers had dug into her.

He had lost control in the end. He'd come as undone as she had. And Riya hugged the fact to herself.

She had known, after all these years of denying herself the simplest touch, it would be strange, weird. But she felt as if she had died and come out alive again.

She gazed at the corridor through which he had walked, his lean frame radiating with tension.

She had broken a rule she hadn't known. That much was clear.

Had it been the kiss? Had it been the way she clung to him? Or had it been her question about it always being that good? Emotions, he didn't do them. She knew that.

But whatever it had been, it was done. In a way, she was glad she had angered him. That left her alone to face what she had done, gave her a reprieve from what she felt around him.

Because nothing, she realized, could take away from the

moment, from the beauty and wonder of what she had experienced. She wasn't going to regret it; she wasn't going to ruin it.

It had been the best few hours of her life, the most alive she had felt. The most fearless she had been. Free to look and touch and taste without wondering about the consequences,

And now it was over.

For a few more seconds, she let herself linger in the moment. Buried her face in the pillow. Breathed in his scent again. Remembered the heady pleasure of being locked under him, her every breath, every moment, every inch of pleasure she felt, all his to give.

Her emotions and herself, under his total control and how good it had felt.

Imagined that he was still there, pulling her into that lean body of his, wrapping those corded arms around her and holding her safe.

This was not a rejection. And even if it was, she couldn't care.

It took only a few moments under the hot spray of the shower for Nathan to realize how heartless he had been. He didn't have to break his self-imposed rules, but he could have at least said a kind word to her. Could have made sure she was okay.

For goodness' sake, it had been her first time.

When had he turned into such a thorough bastard? He felt a distinct unease in his gut. Walking away shouldn't have become this easy. All she'd asked was a simple question.

How could he forget that Riya was new to this, and not just physical intimacy? The hardened cynic that he was, even he'd been moved by the intensity of it.

Wrapping the towel around his hips, he trailed water all over the marble floor as he walked back to the bedroom.

The empty bed felt like a punch to his stomach. He looked around the bedroom and the sitting room and returned to the bedroom again. Her dress was gone. Her sandals were gone. Her clutch was gone.

She was gone.

His phone pinged and he picked it up with a vicious curse. He switched it on, suddenly unsure of where all the anger was coming from. He hated to be so emotional, so unbalanced, and she had done it to him.

"I never asked you to leave," he said.

A short silence reigned before he heard her clear her throat. "I know. I thought it was best. I called to say I found your chauffeur and he's driving me back."

Another silence while Nathan fumed at himself. There was no accusation in her tone. And yet it grated at him.

"Nathan?"

He had taken her virginity and he had forced her into fleeing his bed after the night she had had.

"Nate? Please say something."

Now she sounded wary, tired. And he remembered the emotionally draining day she had had, all thanks to him. "Riya, I'm sorry, I should have—"

"Thank you, Nate," she said, cutting him off. There was no sarcasm or mockery in her tone. Only genuine gratitude.

His throat closed off.

"For...for everything tonight."

"Hell, Riya. You don't have to thank me for sex. I'm not a..."

What? What was he not? And what was he? What was he doing with her?

She laughed, and the ease of the sound only darkened his mood. Had it really been that simple for her? Just been about one night? Had he ruined all her innocence, changed her forever?

"Thank you for being there for me tonight, for your kindness. No one's ever done that for me. No one's ever let it be about me. That's what I meant earlier. I...I will always cherish tonight. And the...sex..."

He had a feeling she was forcing herself to sound breezy.

"...it was more than I would ever have known if left to my own devices. Would never have known how beautiful it could be." Another laugh, self-deprecating this time. "So yeah, thanks for that too, I guess."

He couldn't say a word, couldn't get his vocal cords to work, couldn't manage anything but a stilted silence. He didn't deserve a word she said; he didn't deserve her.

"Good night, Nathan."

She didn't wait for him to speak before she hung up, probably realizing he wasn't going to say anything.

Her face disappeared from his screen, and he clenched his teeth, a soft fury vibrating through him.

He threw his phone across the room, his chest incredibly tight. He sank to the bed and instantly the smell of her, the scent of sex, hit him hard, and he buried his face in his hands. Gulped in a greedy breath.

There was an ache in this throat, something he hadn't felt since his mother told him about his condition.

It was self-pity, it was fear, it was how he felt when his emotions were out of control.

With a curse, he swallowed it back.

No.

She wasn't allowed to do this to him.

No woman was allowed to send him back to being that boy. No woman was allowed to pry this much emotion from him.

With a ruthlessness he had learned to survive without

fear, with the resolve that had turned him from a runaway to a millionaire, he put her out of his mind. Dressed himself and ordered some coffee. Called housekeeping to change the sheets.

He didn't want any reminder of her, of what they had done together, of how he had felt with her beneath him, of how incredibly good the intimacy with her had been. Neither could he focus on how much he wanted to repeat the night, of how he wanted to find her at the estate and sink into her bed, of how much he wanted to hold her slender body in his arms and drift into sleep...

She made him think of Nate Keys, the boy who had been desperately afraid for himself, who wanted to love and live, who wanted to be invincible. But he couldn't be.

He turned on his laptop and went back to being the man he had trained himself to be.

Nathaniel Ramirez—billionaire, survivor and loner.

CHAPTER TEN

OVER THE NEXT couple of weeks, Riya threw herself into the wedding preparations with a rigor that left her with zero headspace. Between her increased responsibilities at Travelogue and the wedding preparations, not to mention the toll it was taking on her to avoid her own mother while living in the same house, it was a miracle she was managing as well as she was.

But she liked it like that. Her days were busy to the point of crammed and when she fell into her bed at night, she was so exhausted that she went right to sleep.

It was only when she was doing some mundane organizational task for the wedding that she found herself thinking of Nathan. She had tried to keep her thoughts free of him. But seeing him every day wasn't conducive to purging him from her mind. After a while, she had just given up.

"Are you well?" he had asked her the following Monday at work, his gaze intent.

She hadn't been able to stem the heat spreading up her neck. "I'm fine," she had said, pleased that she had sounded so steady.

He had tucked her hair behind her ear, clasped her cheek for a moment.

Her heart had thundered in her chest, everything in her yearning to keep his hand there. Because that gesture hadn't been about heat or attraction. It had been about affection, about comfort.

Before she had done anything, however, he had jerked back. He had nodded, looked at her some more and that had been that. And taking his cue, she had thrown herself into work.

Training her mind was still one thing. And absolutely another was her body.

Every time she saw him—either at work or the house, because of course, to her growing annoyance, Nathan apparently couldn't stay away from the house and Robert, she remembered the night they had shared.

Their one night of pleasure. Her one night of freedom from herself. And it was in the most embarrassing and humiliating ways too.

Humiliating because he didn't seem to be facing any such problem. He was back to being the intensely driven slave driver and perfectionist Nathaniel Ramirez. The man really had to have a rock for a heart.

Embarrassing because the memories of that night crept upon her all of a sudden.

The taste of his sweat and skin when she had licked his wrist intruded on her when he extended some papers to her in a meeting full of people. She had stared at his wrist for a full thirty seconds before she grabbed the papers from him.

The velvet hardness of him moving inside her, the stroke of his fingers at her core, the way his spine had arced and the way he had shuddered when he climaxed…she couldn't look at him and not think of what she had let him do to her.

With her late entry into the realm of physical pleasures, she understood her fascination with him. Like how he caught his lower lip with his teeth when he was thinking hard. The way he sometimes placed his palm on his chest and rubbed when he frowned.

But what she missed the most was the man she had come to know. His irrepressible energy around her, his constant teasing of her…now one of them, or both, had erected a wall of politeness. They worked together perfectly, but now they were strangers.

Having finalized the menu once again on the caterer's online website, Riya shut her computer down.

"Riya, I want to speak to you," her mother's voice came from behind her.

Shaking her head, Riya shot out of her chair and grabbed her laptop. "I have nothing to say to you."

"Then why on earth are you doing so much for the wedding?"

"For Robert. I'll do anything for him." Which was why she hadn't packed her stuff and left the estate as her initial impulse had been to do.

Jackie flinched and Riya felt a stab of regret and shock. The fact that anything she said or did could even affect her mom, except in the most superficial way, was a shock in itself. But however hard she tried, she couldn't find it in her to forgive or even forget for a little while.

Her jaw clenching and unclenching, Jackie stopped in front of her, blocking her exit. "I knew it. I knew it from the moment he stepped on the estate that he was going to ruin it all."

Despite every intention not to fall into the guilt trap her mom was so adept at laying, Riya still found herself getting sucked in. "What are you talking about?"

"Nathan. He's doing all this. Robert can't stop talking about him. He wants us to leave the estate without complaint, says we can't have the wedding here anymore because Nathan doesn't want it. And when I argued, he raised his voice to me. Nathan's all he can think about—"

"Robert thought he would never see Nathan again. Can't you be happy for him? For them?"

Because Riya was incredibly happy. For both of them. A little part of her was even envious. Of course, Robert had cared about her. And she was so thankful to him for everything. But the light that came into his eyes when he spoke of Nathan made her a little sad too.

"You're so strong, Riya. Not everyone is so...self-sufficient. I made a bad decision. It doesn't mean I don't love you. You can't give up the estate just because—"

"Are you kidding me, really?"

"I'm telling you the truth. That's what you want these days, right? I love Robert. And yes, I begin to panic when he gets mad at me. Just as I panicked when I thought your father would take you away from me."

Her insecurity was at the root of everything Jackie did. For the first time, instead of helplessness and then anger in the face of it, Riya felt pity for her mother.

"Just because Nathan's back doesn't mean Robert doesn't love you anymore. I don't think it works like that."

"No? Look how he's turned you against me. For years, we've been each other's support, all we've had, Riya. And now, just weeks after he's back, you won't even look at me. All these years of—"

"You were never my support. I was yours. You leaned on me when you shouldn't have. If I've had even a little bit of a carefree childhood, it's because of Robert. And if I've known, even for only a few hours, what it means to live, it's only because of Nathan. So excuse me if I don't—"

"Few hours? What're you talking about?"

At Riya's silence, she became even tenser. "It's none of your business."

Her gaze filled with shock, Jackie shook her. "You slept with him, didn't you? Riya. How stupid are you?"

As dramatic and distasteful as she was making it out to be, Riya refused to let Jackie ruin the most perfect time of her life. "That's grand coming from the woman who fell in love with a married man," she shouted, hating Jackie for reducing her to this.

"At least Robert still stuck with me all these years. Nathan will leave and never look back. He's the wrong man for you."

The fact that Nathan was going to leave was something Riya absolutely refused to think about. But she was aware of it, at the back of her mind, gaining momentum, beginning to rush at her from all sides.

"This has nothing to do with the estate or you, or Robert. It concerns only Nathan and me. No one else. As hard as it is for you to accept it, I have a life. Am going to have a life that's beyond you. I'm leaving after the wedding," she said.

She had been thinking about it, but there was no doubt in her mind now.

She had made to move away when Jackie gave a laugh, and the genuine pity in it rooted Riya to the spot. "Now I see why he insisted. He's planned it all along. And you went straight to his arms."

"What on earth are you talking about?"

"Nathan. He was the one who insisted I tell you about your father. He manipulated you into his bed, Riya. He doesn't care about you."

The urge to slap her hands over her ears was so strong that she dug her nails into her palms. "No," Riya denied, something inside her shaking at the revelation. She closed her eyes and his face, kind and resigned, flashed in front of her. "He didn't manipulate me. He never could." She kept whispering the word, too many things shifting and twisting in front of her.

"He didn't plan anything. He wanted nothing but for me

to know that I was throwing my life away. He's the first person in my life who thought about me, who cared enough to do something about it."

Her mom would never understand. And she needed to be okay with it. It wasn't that she hated Jackie now. Only that she realized that she had a life beyond Jackie, beyond her father, beyond Robert and beyond the estate.

On some level, she knew she should be angry with Nathan. He had been high-handed; he had brought her nothing but hurt. He had set it up without breathing a word to her.

But she couldn't be.

Wasn't it the truth that hurt her? Jackie who had hurt her? Even her father, to some extent, by threatening Jackie to take her away?

Nathan had only liberated her from under the burden of the truth. And then he'd been there to catch her when she was falling. It felt precious, momentous, this molten feeling inside her, this expanding warmth in her chest that he had cared.

She went looking for him later that afternoon when she heard Maria mention that he was visiting. Found him sitting at the gazebo.

He sat with his denim-clad legs stretched in front of him, with his head resting behind him, his face turned up. Sunlight hit his face in rectangular stripes. Kissed the shadows under his eyes. Caressed the planes and hollows of his cheekbones. The breeze ruffled his hair, the copper in it glinting in the sunlight.

His tan was fading a bit and his mouth, not smiling, not teasing, was a tight bow, his lower lip jutting out.

He looked strained, she thought with a pang. He was always such a dynamic, go-go-go, bursting-with-unending-energy kind of man that she didn't like seeing this stillness in him. There was a melancholic quality to that stillness, a dark shadow to the quiet enveloping him.

A sharp need gripped her. Not to feel his touch, although that was there too. But this was a clamoring to reach him, wrap her arms around him, hold him close. For herself, yes, but for him too.

In that moment, there was a loneliness around him. The same one inside her that she had covered up as the need for security.

The realization brought her up short. And she shook her head. It was ridiculous. Just because she felt alone in the world didn't mean Nathan was. It was his choice in life. It had been her choice too, but she hadn't even been aware of it.

As though he could hear her thoughts piling on top of each other, he looked up. His eyes were a different blue in the sunlight, but even the sharp gaze couldn't hide the strain around them.

There was that instant heat between them. He leaned forward onto his knees and frowned. "Is something wrong?"

She shook her head.

For a full minute, she stood there, holding his gaze, not knowing if she wanted to step forward or turn back.

He sighed, a harsh expulsion of breath and anger, she thought. "Come here," he said.

And she went, silencing the clamor inside her. Settled down next to him and stretched out her own legs.

It was a beautiful day with a soft breeze that carried all kinds of fragrances with it. The silence between them, even though a little tense, slowly drifted into a comfortable groove. And she didn't fight it, didn't seek to cover it up or change it.

Was this where they were going to settle? In this place between simmering heat and a strange intimacy?

Slowly she covered the gap between them. Scooted closer until her thigh grazed the hard length of his. Leaned back and sideways until she hit the wall of his chest. Wound her arm around his lean waist. Held herself tight and still, bracing for his rejection.

Seconds piled on top of each other, her breath balled in her throat. He didn't push her away. Her heart thundering just as fast as when she had stripped in front of him, she wrapped her arm around his torso and leaned her head on his chest.

She almost flinched when his right arm came around her shoulders and pulled her closer. Her breath left her in a shuddering whoosh and she settled into his embrace. He smelled familiar, and comforting. He felt like home. And this time, she knew it wasn't the estate. It was the man.

She didn't know how long they sat like that.

"You don't want the wedding to be here?" she finally asked, loath to ruin the peace but needing to. Because if she didn't, she had a feeling she would never let go.

And that was definitely reason to panic.

He tensed, but when he spoke, there was no anger in him. "No."

Feeling his gaze on her, Riya looked up. He ran his thumb over her temple. Pressed a kiss to her forehead. And yet there was no shock in either of them that he'd done it.

Because how could anything that felt so right be wrong?

"I have no anger for her, your mother," he said, and her chest expanded at the kindness in his words, at the rough edge of emotion coating it. "I just want this place to remain my mother's."

Riya nodded, her throat clogging. "Do you miss her very much?"

His mother…she was asking about his mother. The woman who had died with fear in her eyes. She couldn't have jolted him out of the moment better than if she had electrocuted him, reminded him of everything wrong that he was doing. Sitting here, sharing this moment with her, comforting her, finding something in her arms, this was wrong.

All of it, every precious second, every incredible touch.

Nathan jerked away from her and shot up from the bench, fear filling his veins. Every inch of him vibrated with a feral need to ask her to come with him, to show her the world, to have her in his bed for as long as they wanted each other.

And he couldn't let her have this much power over him, couldn't yearn for things he could never have. He steeled himself against her beauty, her heart, and willed himself to become cold, uncaring.

It was the only way to save her from a bigger hurt.

"My manager's taking care of all the arrangements to have the wedding somewhere else. You don't have to redo them. And Robert too. There will be a nurse who will check on him once every day. He and your mother, I'll take care of them, Riya. You've carried their burden long enough."

He had thought of everything. He was making arrangements. Before he… And suddenly she couldn't lock away the questions. "Thanks. So you'll be at the wedding?"

He laughed, and now there was no more easy humor in the sound. The moment was fractured. And she didn't know why. He tucked his fingers into the pockets of his jeans. Looked anywhere but at her. And Riya tried not to show her utter dismay.

It was obvious withdrawal, painful retreat.

"I would like nothing but to leave this very instant and not look back. I've stayed too long already and I'm getting restless. But I did give you my word."

He was not joking and the utter lack of any emotion in

his words shocked her. She had barely made friends, or any other relationship for that matter. And he...he was one relationship she didn't want to lose. "Are we friends, Nathan?"

His jaw tight, he stared at her for several seconds, anger dawning in his gaze. "We are nothing, Riya."

She flinched at the cutting derision in his words. The entire tenor of the conversation had changed. "Why are you acting like this? What did I do wrong?"

"You were fun that night." Her palm itched to knock the derisive curve of his mouth. "Today, you're falling into a pattern that I'm allergic to."

"Because I want us to be friends? I know that it was you that forced Jackie to tell me truth." When he opened his mouth, she put her hand over it to hush him. And felt the contact jolt through her. "I know you did it because you cared. I don't want explanations. I just...I think I would like us to be friends, Nate. I..." She stopped, arrested by the look in his eyes.

"I did what I did because I felt sorry for you, for what your mother and this estate—for what they all did to you."

"Sorry for me?"

"Yes. You manipulated the truth to bring me here, risked everything to patch things up between Dad and me. It has brought me a peace unlike anything. I thought I would pay you back the favor, lift the veil from your eyes, so to speak.

"We're not anything, Riya. We can't even be called a one-night stand. Because you weren't even there for the whole night, right? And we're definitely not friends."

And now she was angry, very angry. And stunned, because there was nothing but finality in his tone. "Why not? Why are you being such a jerk?"

"Because there could be no friendship between us, Riya. Not after that night. When I leave here, you won't see me again, hear from me again. *Ever.*"

Her breath knocked around in her lungs. It didn't feel as though he was stating a fact. It felt as though he was making her a promise. A painful one.

"You never plan to visit the estate that you went to all this trouble for? You'll kick us all out and just let the house be?"

"Yes." The word kicked her in the gut. "I could say otherwise now to make you happy, but it would be a lie. And I can't bear lies."

Something glimmered in his eyes, but Riya had no idea what. He was hurting her with his words. He was aware of it and he was still doing it. Very efficiently even.

Suddenly the cold stranger from the first day was back. Nathaniel Ramirez was back. And the man who had learned more about her in a few weeks than anyone else in her entire life, he was gone.

"Don't do this, Riya. Don't fixate on me because I'm the first man you slept with. Or because I'm the first man who showed a little bit of concern." He clasped her cheek, devouring her as if he were starving, as if he was memorizing every feature, every angle of it. "What you feel for me is only attraction. Only your body asking for—"

"A repeat performance? You think I'm naive enough to sugarcoat my words when all I want is one of those fantastic orgasms you deal out? And for the record, if that's what I wanted, I'm sure you would oblige me, wouldn't you?"

Now there was anger in his eyes. And Riya was glad. She wanted him to be angry, she wanted him to be hurt.

"I think you don't know the difference between a good friend, a great lover and a man who deserves your love. I'm only good for one of those roles. I think you haven't seen enough of the world to know yourself."

"Right. Because Nathaniel Ramirez knows what's best for everyone." She pushed his hand away, hating herself for wanting to revel in his touch. "Will you do me two favors while you're still here, then? Or have I run out of luck with you?"

He looked pale, drawn out. As if there was nothing more left in him. And she was the one who was hurt. "Yes."

"Can you find out where my father is? Put all your power and wealth to use?"

"Yes, I'll put someone on it. What's the second one?"

"There's a week to the wedding. It would make me really happy if you didn't come here. Robert can come see you at the hotel."

"Why?"

Stepping back, she ran her fingers over the wood grain, her throat clogging. "This has been my home for more than a decade. You have the rest of your life here. I only have one week. I want to enjoy it. And if you're around, it'll ruin it for me."

He nodded and then walked away. Riya sank to the bench, her limbs sagging.

For some reason, the tears came then.

They hadn't come so many times when she wished for them, when she needed an outlet for the ache in her heart. They hadn't come when she thought her father had let her go. They hadn't come when she learned that Jackie had lied. But they came now.

Sitting in the gazebo, in the place that had been home to her, Riya cried.

She didn't know why, and she didn't try to understand. Only tucked her arms around her knees and let the tears draw wet paths over her cheeks. She cried for the little girl she had been, for the lost and guarded teenager she had been, for the frozen woman she had become.

She didn't think about Nathan. He had no place in this. This was for her. Only her.

And when the tears dried up and her head hurt, she wiped her cheeks, took a shuddering breath and stood up. Looked around at the lush greenery.

What she had been doing was not enough anymore. That night with Nathan had only been the beginning. Something had to change in her life. She needed to live more. Not that she had any idea how to do that. But she had to start somewhere. After the wedding, she would leave.

She would have to quit her job. She would have to plan her finances, apply for part-time remote-access jobs. To give up all the stability she knew, to leave a job that paid well, the city she had grown up in, to leave Robert and Jackie…the excitement of it all, the fear of it, rocked through her.

There was a whole world out there. And staying still wasn't an option anymore.

Standing at the entrance to the kitchen, Nathan felt every muscle in him clench with a feral ache. Every soft cry that fell from Riya's mouth, every hard breath, landed on him like a claw, raking through him.

But he couldn't go to her. He couldn't hold her as he wanted to, he couldn't promise her that life would get better. That it would hurt less and less. That pain was just as much a part of life as joy.

He didn't make the mistake of thinking she was crying over him. He knew she was saying goodbye. Still, he wished he could be her support even as it was he who was forcing her to leave.

Ask her to come with you, Nate, a voice piped up, catching him unaware.

If he gave in to the longing inside him, if he asked her to come with him temporarily, just until this fire in him was at least blunted… Whether she realized it now or not, when this wave of risk-taking became too much, her natural world would reassert itself. There would be nothing for him except her rejection.

And that rejection would kill him as nothing else had done. To see that fear in her eyes would surely finish him off. And he couldn't blame Riya for being who she was, for the way she had survived.

He would never be the right man for her. And if he wanted to nip this…this yearning, this longing she made him feel, he would have to leave soon. Not risk seeing her again.

Before he forgot, before he started hoping for things that would never be, could never be his. And the distance between hope and fear was not that big.

And so he left, without looking back. As he'd always done.

CHAPTER ELEVEN

THANKS TO THE superefficient event management company Nathan had hired, the wedding preparations went without a hitch. All Riya had to do, even if reluctantly, was to keep her mother calm and turn up to the wedding. More than once, she had indulged in the idea of leaving even before the wedding. But doing that would have hurt Robert and, of course, her mother.

And she wasn't ruthless enough yet just to cut them out of her life.

But the week leading up to it, surprisingly, had been a pleasant one. Grudgingly she accepted that this fact was due to Nathan. She was aware he threw around his wealth as he pleased, but that he had actually cared enough to have the event organized for Robert, that she couldn't overlook.

Since he had kept his word and she had mostly worked from home, she hadn't seen him for the whole week. Having always been the one to take care of the logistics and details of their everyday life, she felt that having it all taken out of her hands had been the best. All she had needed to do was to pick a dress. And even that hadn't been left to her.

She had been presented with three gorgeous ones that a team from a world-famous fashion house, from whose designs she had never been able to afford even a pitiful scarf, had been waiting with for her one afternoon. A stylist and designer along with the dresses.

She had balked at the idea of wearing anything Nathan paid for. Had absolutely refused to even look at the selection picked out for her.

Until he had texted her: Am paying for the wedding. To show my father that I don't resent it.

Can buy my own dress, she had texted back. My boss is a heartless pig, but he pays well.

Thundering silence until…

It's a welcome-to-the-family gift. Accept it or I'll call you sis J

She had laughed, imagined the crinkles he got at the corners of his eyes when he did.

Gross and perverted, that's what you are.

Her heart had run a marathon as she waited. And slammed against her rib cage when her phone pinged again.

Please, Riya.

Her fingers had lingered over her phone's screen. Why? she wanted to ask him. He had rejected her friendship, so why did it matter whether she accepted this from him? Why was he playing games with her? Caring and affectionate one second and a ruthless stranger the next?

In the end, under his relentless will, she had given in. Let them fit her. Fallen in love with the frothy beige silk creation that somehow was almost the same color as her skin and yet stood out against it as if it were made for her.

Whispered sinuously when she moved, outlined her curves without being tacky.

Understated and yet elegant, it had shocked her at how much it suited her, her personality. Not the boring, dowdy clothes she had worn before and not the garish red of her wild night.

But somewhere in between, just perfect for her.

Her hair had been twisted into a sophisticated knot on the top of her head, with soft tendrils caressing her neck and jawline. She had refused the makeup artist's help, however.

The limo that had brought them to the hotel from the estate, the quiet but affluent luxury of the hall they were having the reception in, the delicious buffet—despite all the things clamoring for her awe and attention, despite her heart fisting in her chest with the thought that she was going to leave everything that was familiar to her very soon, Riya couldn't silence her need to see Nathan.

But when she entered the hall, shook hands with friends, he was nowhere to be seen.

And so she waited. Through Robert and Jackie exchanging vows, through their friends toasting them.

She stumbled through her own speech, her eyes still locked on the entrance.

And she waited.

She kissed Jackie's cheek, danced with Robert and only then it dawned on her that her waiting was useless.

Nathan had never planned on attending the wedding.

Riya was fuming when Jackie found her in the quiet corridor that seemed to absorb her anger and the sounds she made.

"Riya." Wary hesitation danced in Jackie's eyes. "I'm so sorry, but this is for the best. Let him go, Riya. It's got nothing to do with you."

Shocked at how perceptive Jackie was being, Riya stared at her. "Please, Jackie. Not today. Just enjoy your day."

"I'm learning, Riya. I've never provided you with security, but I do think of you, worry about you. After all this, you deserve happiness, you deserve someone who'll love you and take care of you for a long time. And Nathan is the last man on earth for you."

Riya didn't like the look in Jackie's eyes. And yet, for the first time in her life, she had a feeling that her mother was speaking the absolute truth. "What do you mean?"

"He doesn't deserve you. Isn't that enough?"

"Just please tell me what you mean."

"He has the same heart condition that Anna had."

Gasping, Riya grabbed the wall behind her. A violent shiver took hold of her, and her teeth chattered in her mouth.

She felt as if someone had pushed her off a cliff and the earth was rising to meet her without a warning, without a safety net.

Anna had been barely into her forties when she died.

No. No. No. It couldn't be true. It couldn't be borne.

Nathan was a force of life.

"I don't have a heart. At least, not a working one."

All the signs had been there right in front of her. That night in his suite, he had almost fainted. Did it happen often? That strap he had worn on his wrist sometimes instead of his watch, it had to be a heart rate monitor.

So many times she had called him heartless, had thrown his mother's name in his face, wondered at how easily he cut everyone out of his life... She shot to her feet and swayed, still feeling dizzy. "I need to see him."

"Riya? What's wrong? You look unwell."

She lifted her gaze to Robert's and swallowed. Tried to rally up her good humor, her strength. Because she had always been strong, hadn't she? They all left, they all deceived her; what else did she have but her strength?

But Nathan hadn't deceived her, hadn't lied to her. In fact, had told her that he would always leave.

"Nathan. Do you know where he is?"

"He went back to the estate. He's leaving in a few hours."

Shock traversed through her, a sudden cold in her chest. "He was here. Today? When? Why didn't he—"

"Yes. But he left just as you and Jackie arrived. Said he couldn't stay any longer. He's leaving tonight."

Let him go, Riya, the part of her that she had painfully trained into place screeched at her. *Let him walk out of your life. End it all before you sink.*

"Oh." It was a miracle Riya managed that, because inside it felt as if someone had pulled the ground from under her. "He didn't even say goodbye, Robert. I… He promised me he would be here tonight." She tried to breathe past the fear and spiraling hurt. "I don't understand any of this. How could I not realize? How could he not tell me? I…"

Wrapping his arms tightly around her, Robert hugged her. And enveloped in the love she had always craved, the lack of which had made her erect a shell around herself, Riya found herself unraveling. One question kept relentlessly pounding against her head.

Why did she care so much?

He had made it clear that they didn't mean anything to each other. Not even friends. Having faced abandonment and rejection all her life, she'd always worn retreat as her armor. She wanted to do that tonight too. But he had left her nowhere to hide.

"I'm sorry it came to this, Riya. But you have to know it has nothing to do with you."

Riya laughed because that was what everyone kept saying. "No?" she said, her voice echoing in the quiet of the carpeted foyer. She was so tired of fighting this, of telling herself that she was strong. "It seems everyone finds it so easy to walk away from me, so easy not to feel even affection for me. So easy to reject me. I hate him for doing this, hate myself for feeling like this. I have to be the stupidest woman in the world—"

Shaking his head, his heart in his eyes, Robert sighed. "It's the way he survives, Riya. He would despise himself if he became like Anna."

"*I don't care* what his reason is. I deserved at least goodbye."

"No, Riya. Wait."

Uncaring of the anxiety in his face, Riya tugged at her arm. Every inch of her was shaking with urgency, the rest of her body scrambling to catch up with her heart. "Let me go, Robert. If he leaves before I can get there, I'll never see him again."

Her throat closed up at the very prospect. "Never again." He'd pretty much promised her that. He'd cut Sonia out like that. And to never see him. "I have to talk to him—"

"Don't make this harder on him."

"What about how I feel?" She screamed the words, wondering how to stem the hurt. She'd been prepared to say goodbye tonight, but knowing what she did now… "I never saw my father again. If Nathan leaves before I see him, if something happens to him, I couldn't bear it, Robert."

It hurt as if someone were ripping out her heart from her chest. Had she and the time they had spent together meant nothing? Hadn't she mattered even a little to him? Shards of hurt and pain splintered through her.

Trembling, she patted her palms down her midriff in a rhythm.

"I'm so sorry, Riya. He had no right to do this to you. I'm sorry I didn't protect you—"

The sob that she had battling rose through Riya and she threw herself into her mom's arms. "He doesn't care, Jackie. He was perfectly willing to walk away…without a word. I wish it didn't hurt so much." She clenched her eyes closed. She couldn't give in to tears now. "This goodbye is just for me. Just for me."

Standing in that softly lit corridor, looking at Robert, who had the exact same eyes as his son, Riya calmed herself down. Her world was changing, slipping from her hands, forever shifting. But even for the fear rattling through her, she couldn't stop.

Only one more night, she reassured herself. Just one more night and she would never think about him again.

"You promised me a dance."

Hearing the soft whisper of her voice, Nathan turned around from the balcony. He hadn't been sure if she would seek him out. With a steely focus, he'd not speculated on whether he wanted her to find him.

Leaning against the wall, he let his gaze rove over her. She looked ethereal tonight, like some beautiful, otherworldly creature come to earth with the express purpose of tormenting him. The beige silk dipped and flared around her lithe body, her hair falling like a silk curtain on one shoulder.

Like a shadow, he had watched her step out of the limo. Hadn't been able to help himself from greedily drinking in her beauty. Had exercised every ounce of will when he saw her gaze wander through the hall, looking for him.

It had taken everything he had in him not to drag her away from the appreciative male gazes and there had been too many of those for his liking. But she wasn't his to protect or even to look at. After so rudely rejecting her small advance for a friendship, after witnessing the hurt flash in those beautiful eyes, he'd known he'd better keep his distance from her.

Not hurting Riya had somehow become the most important thing to him.

"If I remember right, you said you didn't want to dance with me," he said, willing himself to smile. His fingers gripped the railing so tight that the pattern would imprint on his palm. "*Leave Travelogue and go away, forever.* Those were your words."

Something shimmered in her gaze, but for the life of him, he couldn't tell what.

Stepping inside, she closed the door behind her. "I changed my mind. I've decided a lot of things have to change in my life."

"Like what?"

With a shrug, she looked away from him and he saw her chest rise and fall, her spine straighten as though she was bracing herself. For what?

He needed to get her out of here. Before he lost the tenuous thread of his control. Before he forgot how it had felt to have her look at him as if he was her hero, as if there was nothing he couldn't conquer. As if he would always be there for her.

She smiled then. There was fear in that smile, a bravery in it. There was something in her eyes that pulled at him, pierced through him. As if she was fighting to stand, as if she was fighting to keep herself together. And, as it had been from the beginning with her, every atavistic, male instinct in him rose to the fore.

Was she afraid? Of what?

He reached her, lifted her chin, looked into her eyes. "Riya, what is it?"

She shook her head, clasped his wrist, brought his hand closer so that his palm was wrapped around her cheek.

Pressed her mouth to the center of his palm. "I'm quitting Travelogue."

"What?"

"I found a remote-access job. It's a software architect position for a charity based in Bali. A six-month contract."

He frowned, worry for her trumping every other emotion in him. "Bali? Do you even know anyone there? Let me talk to some people I know and get the area checked—"

She shook her head. "No. I'm sure I'll be okay. I've taken care of myself so far, haven't I?"

"Why Bali? Why quit Travelogue?"

"Nothing here…nothing feels enough anymore. This life I've been leading, I want more. I want more excitement, more everything."

"Riya, I don't think you should just up and leave."

"Nathan?"

"Hmm?" He made a sound in his throat, incapable of anything else with her hands moving up his body. Sexual tension and anticipation arced and swelled between them, binding them together.

"A part of me wants to throw caution to the wind and live recklessly. A part of me will always hold me back. You are in between, Nate. Between risk and safety." Her hands clasped his cheek, and she tilted his chin up to meet her eyes. Lust and fire danced in them.

He frowned as her palm pressed against his chest, as if it wanted to confirm the thunderous roar of his heart. The intimacy of the gesture swelled inside him. "What do you want, butterfly?"

"That whole night that you promised me." Stepping back from him, she tugged the zipper of her dress down. With an elegant sensuality that sent lust rollicking through him, she pulled the fabric down, revealing the plump globes of her breasts, pushed it past her hips.

The dress pooled at her feet and she slowly kicked it away. Leaving her voluptuous body in a strapless bra and a thong.

He stepped back from her, only by the skin of his teeth. He couldn't be near her and not take what he wanted. He was painfully aroused, every nerve in him strung to breaking point. It didn't help that he'd had two drinks when he never drank, and now he had a simmering buzz in his head. "No."

She reached him before he could draw another breath. "Yes." She had somehow unbuttoned his shirt and now her palm rested against his hot skin, every line and ridge of it leaving an imprint on him. "You don't have to worry, Nate. I know precisely what I want and what I'll be getting. And come tomorrow morning, I'll bid you goodbye with a smile." Bending, she pressed an openmouthed kiss to his chest, flicked his nipple with her tongue.

Lust slammed at him from every direction.

With a punishing breath, he realized he couldn't send her away. She had come back here, hadn't she? She wanted him, and she owned her desire in a way that reduced him to nothing but heat and hunger.

Maybe with her he would always be weak. With the one woman who needed him to be honorable, strong, maybe he would always be this man who needed more than life had given him, who would always be reduced to the lowest denominator there was of him. Who wanted a few more stolen moments, a few more kisses...

It was exactly as he had feared.

Wasn't that why she was so dangerous to him?

All his armor, all his rules flew out the window when it came to her. She had brought forgiveness into his life. For a few weeks, she had banished the loneliness that was a part of his very bones now. She had brought him peace.

And tonight, it wanted pleasure, hers and his, and it wanted all of her, all night.

So he kissed her. Swallowed her soft gasp. Tasted her with hungry strokes of his tongue, learned her all over again. Drank from her until he was heady with lack of air. He was greedy, he was hot and he didn't grant them both even a breath.

His throat ached; his chest hurt at the sweet taste of her. Her touch, as her fingers wound around his nape, branded him. Her body coiled around his, stamped him forever, owned it, even if she didn't know it. Her breasts grazed him, the taut nipples rasping against his chest like tight buds driving him out of his skin.

And in that minute, he knew he would never again know the touch of another woman, the taste of another woman, the embrace of another woman. His breath harsh, he pressed his forehead against hers, the words rising through him like a tornado that couldn't be contained.

Because, as he had realized all those years ago, it wasn't the fact that his heart didn't work that was the problem. It was that it wanted more than it could ever handle in a lifetime. And all the needs and wants he had suppressed to live his life came rising to the fore when it came to Riya.

Everything he had done, everything he had achieved, felt so small compared to this moment when he couldn't say the words he most wanted to say. They burned on his tongue, fighting to be freed, weighed down on his chest, choking him.

He longed to tell her how much he loved her, how she had forever marked his heart, how she had brought forgiveness to his life, how she had, even if it was only these few minutes that he allowed himself, made him feel.

How alive he felt when he was near her, how much he

wanted to grow old with her, how much he wanted to be the one who would protect her, cherish her, love her.

Their teeth scraped, their tongues tangled. Their breaths mixed and became one. They became one.

The bed groaned as they fell onto it, devouring each other. He pushed his fingers up her thighs until he found her core. Only made sure that she was ready for him. Rubbed the swollen bud there. Let her soft moans surround him.

And she matched him in his hunger, giving as good as she got, digging her teeth into his chest, and there was nothing left in Nate but the desperate need to possess her.

He pushed her legs apart roughly in a frenzy of need. Undid his trousers. Tugged her thong out of the way. Holding her gaze, he entered her in a deep thrust that spoke of his desperate hunger rather than finesse.

Her wet heat clamped him tight, and Nate clenched his jaw to keep the words from spilling out.

Her legs wrapped around his hips; her spine bucked off the bed. She groaned and scratched his biceps with her nails as he pounded into her, only the haze of his approaching climax driving him. He touched the swollen bud at her core, glistening with moisture, calling for his touch.

She exploded around him and he thrust harder, faster, riding the wave of her release, forever changed by her.

His chest still expanding and contracting, he gathered her in his arms and rolled, until she was on top of him. But this time, she shied her gaze away from him and he wondered if she was bracing for his caustic words again. Cursed himself for changing her.

Running his fingers through her silky hair, he pressed a kiss to her temple. Tasted the sweat and scent of her skin. She was all around him, and it was the one place Nate never wanted to leave.

It was a place of belonging, it was home, it was what he

had always wanted in the corners of the heart that he had ruthlessly locked away.

Now, when his heart had found the woman it couldn't have but wanted with so much longing, he knew he would never again look at another woman as a man did.

Because he, Nathaniel Ramirez, apparently was a one-woman man. And he resigned himself to it.

If he couldn't have her, he didn't want anyone. With the realization came desperate need. Tugging her toward him, he pushed her onto her stomach. Breathlessly waited to see if she would protest. Turning her face toward the side, the minx smiled at him. "I'm yours tonight, Nate. To do with as you please."

With a hand under her body, he tugged her up until she was on her hands and knees. Splaying his palm on her lower back, he kissed along the line of her spine. Found the bundle of nerves that was already wet and slick for him.

He plunged his fingers into her and stroked the swollen tissue, a guttural sound escaping him. Felt the shudder that racked her. Bending down, he licked the rim of her ear. "Do you want me to stop, Riya?"

"No, please, Nate. Don't."

And that was all he needed. Holding her hips, he thrust into her. Felt stars explode behind his eyes, felt his body buckle at the waves of sensation.

There was no gentleness left in him. No honor, no control. Only excruciating love for the woman beneath him. It took him every ounce of will he possessed to wait for her before he let his climax take over his body.

Pulling out of her, he turned her face to find her mouth.

The spasms of her climax still rocking through her, Riya shivered, a cold dread pooling in her chest. With his explosive lovemaking, Nathan imprinted himself onto every inch of her, and she felt as if she were drowning in the wake of it.

"Did I hurt you, Riya?" Dragging her close until her skin was slick against his, he pressed his mouth over her temple in a reverent touch. Laced his fingers with hers so tight that a stinging heat rose behind her eyes.

Flushing, Riya shook her head.

"Please, Riya, look at me."

"I'm fine. I just…I think I should go now."

With panting breaths, Riya willed the panic and pain rising through her to abate.

She had meant to say goodbye, thought doing so would give her closure. How could she have left without his touch, his kiss, without feeling his tightly leashed control fray around her one more time? Without feeling the closeness she felt when he made love to her, without feeling the raw edge of his emotion seek her, need her? It was the one time she felt cherished, loved, the one time she felt as though she mattered.

And now she had only dug herself deeper.

She couldn't break down now. If she did she would only end up begging him for another second, another minute, another hour. Of him holding her, kissing her, losing himself in her, of wondering if just another night would make him want her, of eviscerating hope that he would ask her to come with him.

Because another night or a hundred of them wouldn't change him, wouldn't make him care for her. Just as she had a sinking feeling only a lifetime with Nathan would be enough for her. And she couldn't let him see how much he had hurt her. She couldn't bear it if he told her in ruthless words that she was naive and a fool and that he had warned her.

Pushing away from him, she wrapped the sheet around

her nakedness. Picked up the dress she'd discarded in such passion. Padded to the bathroom and splashed water over her face. Swallowed the sharp knot in her throat and sucked in a deep breath.

Even the silky glide of the dress over her skin felt like too much sensation to her hyped-up senses.

Keeping her spine straight, she walked back into the bedroom. Instantly her gaze sought and found him, standing at the French doors, looking up at the sky. It was the darkest of the night, just before dawn. He turned just as she found her clutch.

"Riya, before you go, I know someone in Bali who can—"

"No. I don't want your help. I'd like to get going now," she said, and walked toward the door.

He didn't move or speak. Only stared at her, with that utter stillness of his. His gaze devoured her, a maelstrom of emotions in it.

"Goodbye," she whispered, and turned the knob.

But something in her wouldn't calm down. Adrenaline spiking through her, she felt as if she were standing on a cliff.

"Are you ever coming back, Nathan?" When his mouth tightened, she hurried. "Not for me, don't worry. I know that in the scheme of things I matter very little to you. But for Robert, are you ever going to come back?"

She wished he would lie, wished she could believe him if he did.

"No."

Her stomach lurched, like the time it had on that fantastic ride with him. Only this time, he wasn't going to hold her through it. He was going to let her fall and shatter.

"Dad knows that I won't return." He closed the distance between them, something shimmering in his gaze. "Riya, my leaving has nothing to do with you. Don't make this harder than it has to be."

His words were a soft whisper, but the blaze of emotion in his eyes was unmistakable. And the evidence of his emotion birthed her anger, and it flew through her, an anchor in the drowning storm of hurt and fear.

"Has it become that easy for you, Nathan? Have you become that much of a bastard? Or are you just blind to what you have become?"

His chin reared back as though she had pummeled him with her fists. "I've always warned you that—"

"I know that you have Long QT syndrome like your mom. I know that you fainted and almost died when you were thirteen. I know that that night in the lounge, you almost fainted again. I know that you've cut out every ounce of emotion to survive, that you don't want to go…" Her voice broke. "…go like your mother did. But do you believe you're truly living your life, Nathan?"

"Get out, Riya."

Riya smiled through the tears blurring her vision. They had come full circle. "No, I won't. You pushed the truth on me when I wanted nothing to do with it. You made me hurt, made me feel so much for the first time."

"I already know my truth, butterfly. I've lived with it for more than a decade."

"You think you've conquered your weakness, but you're hiding behind it. You think love makes you weak. You think it'll rid you of your control, leave you at its mercy. You think it will leave you with nothing but fear for yourself and for the ones you love… But you're not your mother, Nathan.

"When I think of what you've achieved, the depth of your generosity…you've allowed yourself everything but happiness. How is it courage if you let it dictate how you live your life? How is it life if it has to be without love?

"You pushed me out of my comfort zone. You made me realize what a sterile life I'd built for myself. When my mother told me about you, I was devastated. I was so scared, Nate. In that moment, if I could erase ever knowing you, I probably would have."

He moved then. Grabbed her arms and hauled her to him. It was like being pulled into a whirlpool of roiling emotions. Like being sucked into the heart of a tornado. "If it scared you so much, then why did you come?"

"I came to say goodbye," Riya said, losing the fight. "I fought the fear that was roiling through me and came to see you. I came despite it, Nathan." She pressed a kiss to his jaw and released the words that she was courageous enough to speak. She knew now he would always plan to leave. But it didn't have to be today. "Tell me not to leave. Ask me to come with you."

Tugging her hands away, he let her go and stepped back. And Riya knew he was putting her out of his mind. "One day, you'll thank me for not taking you up on your offer, butterfly. One day when you find the man who'll love you forever, you'll be glad I left."

CHAPTER TWELVE

Three months later

RUNNING A HAND through his overgrown hair, Nathan waited as the cardiologist checked his heartbeat. It was always hard for him to sit still and even harder when it was this routine checkup.

His chopper was waiting on the roof of the hospital in a remote area of the island of Java. He had stopped seeing world-renowned specialists a long time ago. From day one, he had accepted that there was nothing to be done.

The doctor, who was seeing him for the first time, examined Nathan with warm brown eyes. "You're in remarkably good shape for a man with your condition, Mr. Ramirez," he said in perfect but accented English. "But I guess you know that. Just keep doing what you're doing."

Nathan nodded and thanked him.

"Your next checkup is in—"

"A month," Nathan finished for him.

Thanking the doctor, he was buttoning up his shirt when his cell phone rang. Seeing the face of his virtual manager, he switched it on. "Yes?"

Jacob sounded wary. "Those papers have come back unsigned again."

Nathan caught the fury that rose through him. It wasn't

Jacob's fault. It was that manipulative minx's. What the hell kind of game was she playing? Why was she bent on tormenting him? "From where?"

"From Bali again." So she still hadn't returned. "And there was no reply to our lawyer's question about what she wants."

It had been the same for the last three months. He would send the papers to her and she would send them back, unsigned. Without a reply.

Nathan clenched his teeth, the emptiness he had been fighting for months sucking him in. "Find her number for me."

A few minutes later, Nathan punched in her number and waited. His heart leaped into his throat, his pulse ringing very much like the peal of the phone on the other line.

"Hello?" her voice came across the line, and his stomach lurched. Just hearing her voice was enough to drive him into that crazed, out-of-control need to see her, to touch her, to hold her close, to wake up to her face.

"Hello?"

Stepping back from the sunshine, Nate leaned against the brick wall. Took a deep breath. "Why the hell aren't you signing the papers, Riya? What do you want now?"

The line was silent for a few seconds. And her face popped up in his mind's eye, her expression stricken as she had left him that night.

"I… Nate, how are you?"

"I'm alive, Riya." He heard her gasp and ignored it. At least now there was no need to pretend. "And if I weren't, you would be the first one to—"

"Bastard."

This time, he laughed, chose again to ignore the cutting pain packed into the single word. "Cut the theatrics and tell me why you're refusing to sign away the estate."

"I decided that it should be mine. That I don't want to part with it, after all."

Disbelief roared in his ears. And he let a curse fly. "Have you finally decided to listen to your mother, then?"

"I figured it was mine every which way it counted," she continued smoothly, as though he hadn't just insulted her and *this thing between them*, as though she wasn't tying him up in knots.

"And how did you come to that impossible conclusion?"

"Robert, who's my father as far as I'm concerned, deeded it to me with love. I'm strong enough to accept my right over it now. Of course, that's thanks to you. And more than that, I figured it was mine because it belonged to the man I love with all my heart."

He felt as if a fist had jammed up into his chest. He couldn't breathe as her words sank in. There was no hesitation in her voice. "You've lost your mind," he said, pushing the words out through a raw throat. "Gone over the edge."

"Actually it's the opposite. I've realized that my happiness is in my hands. Not Jackie's or Robert's or even yours. That I have to believe that I deserve love. That I have to risk pain to fight for it." Now she didn't sound that put together. "Admit it, Nate. If I asked you for it right now, you wouldn't fight me. You wouldn't deny me."

His butterfly was getting reckless, coming into her own. Despite the ache in his heart, he smiled. "Why would I do that?"

"Because you love me." She waited, as though she wanted him to feel the full impact of her outrageous announcement. "You can put thousands of miles between us, you can cut all connections from me, you might never even see me again. But you think about me all the time. That estate, that massive fortune of yours, that faulty but generous heart of yours…they are all mine."

"You sound very sure, Riya."

The sound of her laugh pierced through him. "I think I know you as well as I know myself now. I realized that I won't ever have to work a day in my life again and still live like a princess. Because one of the richest and the most wonderful man in the world…I belong to him now. How's that for security, huh?"

She sounded confident, even brazen, but he could imagine the tears in her eyes, her hands fisting at her sides as she forced the words past that beautiful mouth. "But the thing is, I would rather risk my heart for another moment with him than have all the security in the world." He heard her suck in a breath. "That estate is the best waiting place for me when I come back."

With every word she said, she was twisting his insides, unraveling him. And beneath his rules, his honor, his revulsion for fear, Nate saw something else. As if he had been sitting in the dark all this time, mistaking his cowardice for his guts.

He asked the question he knew he shouldn't. "Waiting for what?"

"For you to come home." The ache in her voice was as clear as the ache in his own heart. "For you to come back to me." And she was crying and unraveling, right along with him, even though there were thousands of miles between them.

He rubbed his eyes with his fingers, a stinging heat prickling behind them. Her words gouged a hole through the emptiness he felt. "That's never going to happen, butterfly. You're wasting your precious life. You want a stable life with a steadfast man who'll be with you for the rest of your life, remember? Me? I could be gone any time." His own cheeks were wet now and Nathan didn't feel ashamed or afraid, only ache.

"Yeah, well, you ruined all my plans for my life, Nate. Now I want something else."

"Yeah? What?"

"A decade, a year, a day, or even another moment with the man I adore. With the man who showed me how to live, and love. With the man I'll love for the rest of my life."

He heard her grasping breath, the catch in her voice. Heard her tear-soaked voice as if she were looking at him with those beautiful brown eyes.

"I love you, Nate, with every breath in me. I have been a coward all my life. I was a coward even that night. I let you walk away. But not anymore. I deserve happiness and so do you. My life is empty without you, Nate."

How he wanted to believe her; how he wished he had the courage to be the man she deserved. Because that was what he was lacking. Not the robust heart, not a body that would live for a century. But the courage to grab the love she offered, to trust her love and his, to risk his heart.

Whatever it was that was holding him back now, protecting his heart, this was fear.

He was in that moment he had dreaded his whole life. Fear and pain. And yet it was of not seeing Riya ever again, of not waking up to her, of not seeing her wide mouth split into a smile at the sight of him, of not holding her tight until they couldn't breathe.

"I'm waiting for you, Nate." She was crying now, in soft sobs and broken words. And the pain that caused him was more than any he had ever felt, hurt deeper than any other fear that he didn't want to feel.

"I think I'll always wait for you."

And then she hung up.

Riya sank to her bed in her hotel room, her breaths coming jerkily. Grabbing the edge of the T-shirt she had taken from Nate that night, she buried her face in it. Every inch of her was still vibrating at hearing his voice. Her fingers hurt with how tightly she had fisted them, how she wanted to touch him, feel his arms around her.

Had he known that she was falling apart? How much it had cost her to say what was truly in her heart, even knowing that it might never change his mind? How big a risk she had taken by binding herself to him, by giving him her heart?

But to this new Riya whom he had brought to life, nothing less than what she wanted, what she deserved was acceptable.

Without him, nothing in the world meant anything to her.

CHAPTER THIRTEEN

NATHAN FOUND HER a month later on a beach in Ubud, Bali, in one of the villas RunAway owned, sitting on the deck that offered spectacular views of rolling hills and valleys. The villa was the utmost in privacy and comfort. It perched atop a valley overlooking a lush river gorge.

It had been his very own slice of paradise. When Jacob told him that a request had come in from his property manager that a woman named Riya *Ramirez*, who'd claimed to be his close friend, had wanted to use it, he had laughed for a full minute. The woman was relentless, stubborn, manipulative, and he loved her for all of it.

And yet, with the setting sun casting golden shadows on her striking face, it was loneliness that enveloped her now. And it clawed at his heart.

It had taken him three weeks to consolidate his worldwide holdings, to find and hire efficient managers where he needed, to fight the voice that whispered *no* every second of the day.

But there had also been one that kept counting the time down, telling him that he had wasted enough as it was. And he realized, if he had lived without fear, he had also lived without joy for too long.

Once he had decided, it had taken him a week to find her, and every minute of waiting to hear more had been excruciating. Until the stubborn woman herself had sent him a clue.

Did she love him that much? Would she have stopped at nothing until she got through to him? Could he always prove himself worthy of it?

Feeling a knot of anxiety, he clenched and unclenched his fingers.

She was dressed in a sleeveless, floral dress that rippled around her knees with the breeze.

"Riya?" he said, unable to say anything else past the emotion clogging his throat.

She was off the lounging chair and deck before he could blink. Standing before him with her hair flying in her face before he could draw another breath. Her chest falling and rising, her mouth pinched.

And the love in her eyes undid Nathan as nothing had ever done. "I love you, butterfly," he said, and she swayed, a gasp falling from her lips. Threw herself into his arms like a gale of wind. Knocked the breath out of him, knocked him off his feet.

He buried his mouth in her neck, filling himself with the scent of her.

Her arms wound around him so tight that he laughed. Pulling her head back, she glared at him. "I'm never letting you go, ever. You even talk about leaving me again and I'll chain you to myself." A shudder swept through her in direct contrast to the bravado in her words.

"I love you so much, Nate. I've missed you so much. Every day, every night, wherever I want, I thought about you. It hurt so much that I wanted it to stop for a while. It felt like—"

"Like you were missing an essential part of yourself?" he said, and she nodded.

He tasted her in a rough kiss, needing the fortification,

needing tangible proof of her taste. She clung to him with just as much desperation.

"Do you know what you're signing up for, butterfly?" he said, when his desperation had blunted, when his heart beat normally again. When the shadow of a lifelong fear clasped him tight. "It would kill me much sooner to see—"

Her palm closed over his mouth and she shook her head. "I do feel fear, and sometimes I can't breathe thinking of this world without you. But I'd rather fight that fear every day than live another moment without you. I'll do it, Nate. I'll only ever try to be your strength. And all I ask is that you give me the chance. To love you, to be loved by you, for as long as possible, that's all I want."

Clasping her hand in his, he dragged her to the edge of the deck and looked out into the valley and beyond. Turned her toward him and dropped onto his knees.

"I love you, Riya, with every breath in my body, with every beat of my faulty heart. I was so lonely before I met you. I thought I was protecting you by walking away. When you called me, when you so bravely put into words what you felt for me...to hear you say what I felt for you, to hear you tell me you chose to love me even as you were afraid, it made me realize I wasn't living, merely existing. You've taught me what it is to be brave, butterfly."

Riya kissed him, tears stinging her cheeks. Running her hands over him greedily, she clung to him, fear and joy all bubbling inside her. Her biggest risk had paid off and her heart stuttered in her chest. "All I want is to be by your side for the rest of our lives."

His eyes shining with unshed tears, he kissed her temple. "Will you be my wife, butterfly? Will you tie yourself to me, then?"

Riya nodded, the small doubt in his tone doing nothing to abate the intensity of her own love. He had come for her;

he had shown her his heart. It didn't mean years of protecting himself from fear and hurt would be gone this very second. But she was strong enough for both of them. "Yes."

He dragged her into the cradle of his arms, his lean frame shuddering. "That's the sweetest word I've ever heard, Riya."

For the first time in his life, Nathan felt joy, and he felt complete. With the woman he loved with him, there was no place for fear.

Only love and utter happiness for the rest of his days.

EPILOGUE

One year later

HIS BREATH HITCHING in his throat, every inch of him thrumming with anticipation, Nathan turned around and froze.

With the blue sea and white sand as her background, Riya stilled beneath the arch that was decorated with sheer white lilies and cream-colored silk.

Her gaze met his, her mouth wreathed in a shy smile; she was waiting to see his reaction, he realized.

The red sheer silk sari she wore wound around her striking figure, baring her midriff, inviting his touch. When he had looked at the huge yard of the material and frowned a week ago, she had patiently and laughingly explained to him how it worked, and how much fun she was having with her aunt teaching her how to wear it.

And that she was learning it for him, she had said with a wink.

He was glad she did.

The silk draped over her left shoulder and hung behind her, hiding and showcasing her beautiful body. Her long hair flew in the breeze, but it was the glittering expression in her eyes that arrested him.

He couldn't breathe when he remembered her tears when they'd learned that her father had passed away a few years before they'd tracked him down. He had held her all night, her pain as much as his. And the smile in her eyes, when he'd told her about the aunt his PI had located… the only blood relative of her father still alive.

All his wealth and power, he had truly appreciated it that day. For it had brought such happiness to the woman he loved.

He mouthed, *I love you* and tears shimmered in her gaze as she walked toward him.

Her heart racing as if toward some invisible goal, Riya rubbed her fingers over her face. She blew out a breath, a shadow of fear marring her perfect day.

Beneath the cliff on top of which the villa sat, the sea was dark blue, the horizon where the sky met the sea not visible. It was the most beautiful place she had ever seen.

The wedding on the beach had been her dream come true. Robert, Jackie and her aunt, and the staff from the estate, Riya had never felt more loved or cherished.

And in between all of it was the man she loved.

It had taken all these months for Nathan to believe that she truly wanted this—that she wouldn't change her mind, that she would never stop loving him, that she would never let herself be driven by fear.

And now the truth she had realized just this morning.

Wrapping her arms around herself, she battled both excitement and fear.

She turned when the door of the main bedroom in the villa closed with a soft thud.

Nathan stood leaning against the door, and the raw heat in his eyes instantly sent an answering tremble through her. She wondered if she was betraying herself, if the small thing she had learned this morning was written on her face.

"I don't want you to wear a sari again."

"What?" She ran her hands over the silky folds, distracted by his expression. "You don't like it?"

"As your husband, I command you not to wear it in public," he added with a possessive glint in his eye, and she laughed.

"I've been waiting to say that since I saw you walking down toward me."

He caught the edge that trailed over her shoulder with one hand and tugged hard. And the silky soft material came undone around her and ripped at her waist.

He tugged until Riya was caught in his arms.

"You look utterly gorgeous and scandalously sexy in it. And I don't want any other man but me to see that."

He buried his mouth in the curve of her neck, his hands settling around her bare midriff. "Nate, wait, I want to—"

"It's all I've been wanting to do since I saw you, Riya. Please don't deny me."

Forgetting her own words, she pushed into him and sank her fingers in his hair.

As he whispered words that made her core pulse with spiraling need, his long fingers climbing up her midriff toward her breasts encased snugly in the blouse.

He groaned and pulled the hooks that held it together with a strong tug and Riya gasped as she heard the blouse rip at the hooks. With impatient fingers, he pushed the cups of her bra down.

She shuddered as his abrasive palms covered her breasts, the aching, tight nipples rasping against the roughness. Rubbing her buttocks against his hard body, Riya loosened the petticoat and let it pool at her feet.

His palms moved over her waist and then her thighs. When he picked her up and placed her on an exquisitely crafted sofa table, she laughed and gave herself over to the dark passion lighting up his eyes.

Their lovemaking was swift, desperate, coated with the awareness that they were now joined in the holiest of bonds, exalted by the promises they had made to each other. Sweat cooling on her forehead, she leaned her head against his chest, the superfast rhythm of his heart comforting under her palms.

She kissed the taut skin of his pectorals, breathing in the musky scent of him.

"You always do that," he said, his words a gravelly rasp against her senses.

Looking up, she smiled, her arms still around him. "What do you mean?"

He pushed sweaty tendrils of hair that stuck to her forehead. "Check my heart. Every time after we make love, you put your face to my chest as though you want to—"

Shaking her head, she put her fingers over his mouth. "I'm sorry, I didn't even realize that I did that. I didn't mean to make you feel—"

He laughed and swallowed the rest of her words in a sizzling kiss. "These last few months have been the happiest of my life. Every day, I can't imagine this is my life. I can't believe that I walked away from this. If you hadn't fought for me, for our love..." He sighed against her mouth, a shudder racking through him. "I love you, Riya. I love that you'll forever be mine and I yours."

An ache rose in Riya's throat at his words. Her gorgeous, powerful man never let a day pass without telling her how much he loved her, without showing her how precious she was to him. But they were both still so new to this. He was only now getting used to having her around after living alone for so long.

Underneath that easy humor, there was still a self-sufficiency that wouldn't leave so easily. But he made an effort for her and Riya was so glad for it.

Hiding her face in his chest, Riya gathered the courage to say the words. "Nathan, I have to tell you something."

"What is it, butterfly?"

"I realized yesterday that…I…we've been traveling so much and I lost track of…"

He lifted her chin, his gaze curious. "What's bothering you?"

"I took a pregnancy test this morning, and it's… I'm pregnant, Nate."

Shock flitted in his eyes, cycled to concern. "I don't know what to say."

Riya felt the happiness of her day pop.

"Riya, I know this isn't what we had planned. I mean, we didn't really even plan anything, did we? But, my little butterfly, that's how you came into my life, didn't you?" He tugged her toward him and hugged her so tight that Riya thought she would break under the avalanche of his love. Yet when he spoke, there was a restraint in his voice. "I know it's scary when we're so new to each other. I know that having a child is a huge thing, but, Riya—"

Riya pushed at his shoulders and studied his gaze. He was holding back his reaction for her. She pulled his hands to her stomach and spoke past the raw ache in her throat.

"Please, Nate. Will you be honest with me about this?"

He nodded and clasped her cheek. "It's the perfect gift you could have given me today. You'll have me every step of the way. You—"

And that was when Riya understood. And she laughed and hugged him tight, kissed his face. Looked into his beautiful blue gaze.

"Nathan, you and I made this. We created this with our love. Can you imagine anything more beautiful or wonderful in this world? It's true I'm afraid, I'm nowhere near ready or equipped to be a mom, but if you're with me, I can do anything. Tell me you want this just as much as I do. Tell me you want this baby."

Tears pooled in his beautiful blue gaze and he kissed her again. Now it was he who trembled and Riya hugged him hard to herself. "I do want this, Riya. I'll always want anything you bring into my life, butterfly."

* * * * *

MILLS & BOON®

Why not subscribe?
Never miss a title and save money too!

Here's what's available to you if you join the exclusive **Mills & Boon Book Club** today:

✦ *Titles up to a month ahead of the shops*
✦ *Amazing discounts*
✦ *Free P&P*
✦ *Earn Bonus Book points that can be redeemed against other titles and gifts*
✦ *Choose from monthly or pre-paid plans*

Still want more?
Well, if you join today we'll even give you
50% OFF your first parcel!

So visit **www.millsandboon.co.uk/subs**
or call Customer Relations on **020 8288 2888**
to be a part of this exclusive Book Club!